THE U

Seated on a stump at the clearing's border, Hawken across his thighs, Nate stared out over his private domain. This valley was his home. Eighteen years earlier he'd claimed it for his own and held onto it, defying repeated attempts by the Utes and others to drive him out. In all that time, none of the threats he faced were as unnerving as this new one.

Confronting a known enemy was one thing, confronting an elusive foe who defied his every attempt to track it down, another. Nate had no notion of who or what he was up against, and it was that, more than the absence of wildlife and the terrified horses, that disturbed him most. How could he protect his loved ones when he had no clue what he was protecting them from? How could he defend his domain when it had been invaded by a will-of-the-wisp?

A destructive will-of-the-wisp. An adversary who grew increasingly brazen, as the shredding of his son's shirt demonstrated. How long, Nate fretted, before the skulker in the forest vented its violent urges on people instead of objects? How long before someone he cared for was harmed?

Soft footsteps jarred Nate's thoughts. . . .

Mountain Nightmare

David Thompson

LEISURE BOOKS NEW YORK CITY

To Judy, Joshua, and Shane.

A LEISURE BOOK®

December 1999

Published by

Dorchester Publishing Co., Inc.
276 Fifth Avenue
New York, NY 10001

ISBN 0-8439-4656-3

Printed in the United States of America.

Mountain
Nightmare

Chapter One

Old Charlie Walker had lived in the Rockies for the better part of thirty years. Not quite as long as Shakespeare McNair and a few of the other old-timers, but long enough to qualify him as one of the most experienced mountaineers alive. Old Charlie had trapped every creature under the sun. He'd lived with half a dozen Indian tribes and knew the ways of the red man as well as any white ever could. He'd endured icy winters without end, inferno summers without cease.

In short, Old Charlie had pretty much seen and done it all. There wasn't much that surprised him anymore, which made it all the more remarkable when he shuffled down to the gurgling stream near his cabin for a drink early one morning and saw some strange tracks.

Charlie had eased onto his aching knees, placed a hand flat, and was bending forward to dip his grizzled chin into the sparkling water when he noticed the prints to his left. He stared at them a moment and thought to himself, *No, that can't be*. Then he slaked his thirst.

Some men were partial to scalding hot cups of coffee, or even tea, first thing every day. Not Old Charlie Walker. Give him fresh, clear, cold water, and lots of it.

When Old Charlie raised his dripping jaw, the tracks were still there. He stared at them some more, completely confounded. They defied all logic. They were as out of place as a grizzly's tracks would be in the heart of New York City.

Sitting back, Old Charlie wiped his mouth with the back of a gnarled hand. Buckskin covered his lanky frame from head to toe and a beaver hat that had seen better days was perched on his gray mane of hair.

"Well, I'll be," Old Charlie said aloud. Talking to himself wasn't unusual. Many of his kind picked up the habit of voicing their thoughts. The sound of a human voice lessened their loneliness a trifle. Charlie was unique in that he held whole conversations with himself, and had once punched himself in the nose when he angrily disagreed with an idle comment he'd made. "What do you have to say about this, hoss?"

"I don't rightly know," he answered himself. "Damned peculiar, is what it is. If'n I didn't know any better, I'd swear someone was playin' a trick on me."

"Who'd be that ornery?" He could think of a few: McNair, that rascal Joe Meek, Running Elk, possibly, and maybe Striped Wolf of the Crows. But it would be a lot of trouble to go to, whittling the feet and—

Old Charlie bent low, his brow knitting. "Hellfire!" he exclaimed. They weren't impressions made by carved wood. *They were real!* He saw where the toes had splayed when the maker of the tracks shifted position. And again, where the toes dug in for purchase as the figure climbed the bank.

"I must be drunk," Old Charlie said. "Yet I can't be. I ain't had a drop of rotgut since I visited Bent's Fort back in—" He stopped, unable to recollect exactly when that had been. Seven years ago? Ten?

His curiosity mounting, Old Charlie rose and followed the tracks. They paralleled the stream for another thirty yards, giving his small cabin a wide berth, then veered into dense forest. Old

Charlie stopped, unsure whether to go on or fetch his rifle and possibles bag. All he had with him was a pistol and a Green River knife.

There was a time when Old Charlie never ventured ten steps from his place without being fully armed. But the Blackfeet and Bloods hadn't been spotted in his neck of the woods in a coon's age, and he'd skinned the last griz on that particular mountain back in '32. He considered it safe to go a little farther.

Advancing in among the pines, Old Charlie heard a chipmunk chitter and a sparrow sing. Proof that no predators were abroad, four-legged or otherwise.

The ground was hard here, so the prints were much more difficult to find. The impressions and scuff marks were so faint, in fact, that if Old Charlie hadn't known what to look for, he'd never have spotted them. It made him wonder if he had blundered by other such tracks in the past and just not realized it.

"This reminds me of that time up in the Tetons," he commented. "When I was with Yellow Hand's band, and we came on those gigantic footprints left by something none of us had ever heard tell of." He paused. "Only, these here weren't made by the same critter, were they, you fool?"

"Who are you callin' a fool?" Old Charlie demanded.

The tracks wound steadily deeper into the woods. At a clearing no wider than Old Charlie was tall, he drew up short in amazement. "If this don't beat a pig a-pecking!" A new set of tracks joined the first, coming from the west. Then both sets headed off side by side.

"Must be the missus," Old Charlie joked, and guffawed. Everything on God's green earth had a mate—but two of these things was as beyond belief as the existence of only one. "I reckon I'll keep on a little ways yet."

The prints bore toward a ravine, a narrow, boulder-strewn defile barely wide enough for four horses to ride abreast. With the sun perched on the horizon, scant light penetrated. Enough, though, to reveal that the tracks were luring him into its murky recesses.

"I reckon I'll come back later," Old Charlie announced. But

he couldn't resist venturing in. *Just twenty or thirty feet or so*, he told himself. It wasn't quite as dark as he'd believed, and he had no trouble trailing the tracks as they wound farther and farther along until he came to a cleft on his right. The footprints disappeared into it.

"That's that," Old Charlie said, since he surely couldn't follow any farther. He'd have to dig for a month of Sundays, and even then he had no inkling of how far back the cleft ran. Stooping, he put his face to the opening and felt a soft, cool breeze on his skin. "It's a deep one, no doubt about it."

Old Charlie started to uncoil, then froze. Something had *moved* back in there. He was certain. Peering intently, he saw the thing move again, a swift, flitting motion. A vague shape materialized, too indistinct to note details. It was there, and it was gone.

"I know you're in there!" Old Charlie informed them. The likelihood of being in any danger never occurred to him. Not given his size, and the pistol. "Step out so I can get a good look at you!"

Nothing happened, and Old Charlie scratched his chin. "It could be they're afraid of me," he guessed. "It could be they think I'll smash them to pieces, or keep one of 'em as a pet." Which wasn't as crazy a notion as it seemed. A friend of his had tamed a wolverine once, impossible as that sounded. Caught a young one and hand-fed it until it was old enough to fend for itself. Damned if the vicious critter didn't like to visit his friend now and again, and eat jerky right out of the jasper's palm.

"Howdy, there," Old Charlie said, smiling to show his good intentions. "I'm as peaceable as a parson. So don't be scared none."

More movement ensued. The shape reformed, slightly to the left. Glittering pinpoints marked its eyes. *Reflection of the light*, Old Charlie figured, but couldn't understand how they gleamed so brightly when there wasn't enough light back in there to read by. His smile widened. "Come on out. Show yourself. I've a hankerin' to be your friend, if'n you'll let me be."

Another pair of gleaming eyes flared in the darkness. Old Charlie's didn't much like how they slanted, or how reddish they glowed. But he wasn't one of those people who disliked something just because it was different.

"I've got some vittles back at my place," Old Charlie mentioned. "Killed me an elk last week, and there's plenty left. How'd you like a nice, juicy haunch? With wild onions and dried berries?"

Charlie's own mouth watered at the prospect. He hadn't had breakfast yet and was starved to death. "Come on out of there. Or at least a little closer so I can see you better."

None of the blazing eyes budged.

"I'm as poor as Job's turkey, but I don't mind sharin'. How about it?"

To Old Charlie's astonishment, a third set of eyes blossomed. "Tarnation!" he blurted. "You're worse than rabbits!"

A trilling filled the cleft, a sound the likes of which Old Charlie had never heard, low-pitched and eerie, like the caterwauling of a painter late at night, only with a lot of hissing and growling mixed in. Old Charlie didn't like it one bit.

"I've tried to be civil, but you're wearin' my patience thin. Either show yourselves or I'm leavin'."

Nothing happened.

"Suit yourselves," Old Charlie said, greatly disappointed. He'd have loved to see them so he could brag about the encounter on his next visit to the Shoshones or Crows. The former, especially, would find it mighty interesting.

All of a sudden, with no logical explanation, the red eyes vanished.

"Rude critters," Old Charlie muttered, rising. His joints objected, and he had to stretch to relieve a kink in his spine. "Reminds me of the time I visited the Piegans. Middle of the winter, yet not a one would see fit to admit me to their lodge."

Enough is enough, Old Charlie mused, tramping away. He glanced over a shoulder every so often on the off chance the creatures were trailing him. No such luck. However, soon the sensation of being watched crept over him, which he blamed on

11

his nerves. Striding into the open at last, he breathed a sigh of relief and bent his legs homeward.

The sparrows had stopped singing, and the chipmunks no longer chattered. Old Charlie paused several times to scour the vegetation, but if the things were out there, they were keeping exceptionally well hidden. "Reminds me of the Sioux, how they sneak around like specters," he remarked.

Old Charlie wasn't worried. He had the pistol, and compared to the creatures he was as big as Goliath. He could stomp them to a pulp without half trying. Tittering at the notion, he ambled to within sight of his cabin. As soon as he emerged from the trees, his mule started acting up, braying and kicking her hooves as if a silvertip were in the vicinity. "Behave yourself, Martha!" he scolded, afraid she'd bust out of the corral and he'd have to chase her down. The last time she broke out, it'd taken him four days to find her. Mules could be downright ornery when they wanted.

Martha kept braying and kicking. As he approached she came to the rails, her long ears pricked toward the forest, her gaze fixed at a point beyond him.

Old Charlie spun. For a fleeting instant, so fleeting he was uncertain whether he saw what he saw, a face seemed to be framed between a couple of bushes, a face so grotesque, so completely and utterly inhuman, that a shiver involuntarily rippled through Charlie and he took a step backward in alarm. Just like that, the face was gone, as if it had never been, leaving him to question whether it had been there or had merely been a trick of the shadows.

"I wasn't brought up in the woods to be scared by owls," Old Charlie tried to assure himself, but he was glad when the cabin door was shut and barred and he was safely seated at the crude table he had built with his own two hands, chomping on some of the elk meat, throwing it down his gullet cold.

"I reckon I'll be jumpin' at my own shadow next," Old Charlie said. "My days are numbered, sure enough." Being skittish was yet another sign he was on the wane. His strength was nowhere near what it had once been, his muscles and bones sore more frequently than they weren't. And just the other day he'd gone outdoors without putting on his moccasins, the first time in his whole life he'd forgotten.

Old Charlie decided to stay close to the cabin the rest of the day. He tinkered with a broken trap, worked at mending a torn pair of britches, and in the middle of the afternoon gathered enough firewood to last a month. As the sun dipped toward the emerald western peaks, a knot of anxiety formed in his gut, apprehension he couldn't shake no matter how hard he tried. Toward evening he watered and fed Martha, and by sunset he had the front door barred and the shutter drawn over the only window.

Snug as the proverbial bug, Old Charlie kindled a fire in the stone fireplace and placed a pot of elk stew on to boil. Soon the fragrant aroma filled the room. He hunkered over the pot, poking at chunks of meat, eager for them to get done. As he waited, he whistled a bawdy tune common in taverns.

Supper was Old Charlie's favorite meal. It meant his work was done for the day and he could relax until sleep claimed him, along about midnight, usually. From a cupboard next to the window he took a tin bowl and a silver tankard he'd brought clear from Missouri, an heirloom that had belonged to his grandpa. Setting them on the table, he rummaged in a drawer for his spoon, a battered implement that had seen almost as many winters as he had. He rarely used it anymore, but tonight he had an urge to eat like civilized folks.

Ordinarily, Old Charlie liked to wash his food down with black coffee. Tonight, to help quell his nerves, a stronger brew was called for. In the far corner was a section of planking that lifted when pulled, and under it, in a hole over a foot deep, was Old Charlie's precious hoard, the last of his ale. He'd meant to save it for a special occasion. But now he filled the tankard to the brim and left the jug on the table.

Except for the crackling of flames, the cabin was quiet as Old Charlie filled the tin bowl and plopped himself down. He ate with relish, treating himself to a swallow of ale every few bites. "This is as good as life gets,'' he commented to the four walls.

A warm feeling spread outward from Old Charlie's stomach, filling him with a sense of well-being and contentment. Belching, he sat back and patted himself. All his fears seemed so silly, all his anxiety so much mist. He would fill his pipe and have a smoke later, then turn in and sleep like a newborn until morning.

Old Charlie grasped the spoon and lowered it into the stew. It was halfway to his mouth when the sensation of being watched came over him again, a sensation so intense and overpowering that he dropped the spoon and jumped to his feet, nearly upending the chair. A glance showed the door and window were both shut tight, and he chided himself for being foolish.

''I'm gettin' worse than a cat on a porch full of rocking chairs,'' he quipped. He resumed eating, lading heaping portions of meat into his mouth and chomping like a starved lynx.

The warmth, the meat, the ale, they all restored Old Charlie's happy mood, and he hummed as he walked to the fireplace for a second helping. He was leaning toward the pot when a skittering noise behind him stiffened him so abruptly, he rapped his skull on the fireplace. Pain spiked him, and as he turned, the room spun like a child's top.

''What on earth—?'' he mumbled. It had sounded like a mouse, but that couldn't be. All the gaps between the logs had been plugged, and his floor was solid planking from end to end. He'd obtained the boards in trade from settlers bound for the Oregon country, fools who overloaded their wagons and had to dispose of half their belongings shortly after crossing South Pass. It'd taken a heap of work, but he was one of the few mountaineers who could boast a solid floor.

He saw no mouse. Angered by the knock on his noggin, he drew his Green River knife and moved toward the wood he had brought in earlier. It was possible he'd accidentally brought a mouse inside, too, maybe concealed in a hole or some such. If so, he'd skewer it and add it to the pot. Mice didn't have much meat on them, but they had a nice flavor.

A search of the pile yielded no rodents. Mystified, Old Charlie sheathed his knife and filled the tin bowl. The pot was close to bubbling over, so he took it off the fire and deposited it on the counter.

"So what if my mind's startin' to go?" he said to the buffalo head mounted on one wall. "I can last another ten years or better if'n I take real good care of myself. No whiskey, no women. Well, maybe just a nip now and then, and a poke every six months or so."

The buffalo's shriveled sockets gazed lifelessly back. Old Charlie had once seen a mounted head in a high-priced eatery in St. Louis, complete with horns and glass eyes. His trophy had the horns intact, although they drooped, but glass eyes were as scarce as hen's teeth west of the Mississippi, so he'd had to go without.

"What's that? You'd like to poke a cow? You stupid critter. Your oysters were part of the feast those Flatheads threw together for the whites who helped them on that surround. Your pokin' days are long over, friend."

Cackling, Old Charlie raised the spoon once more—and that awful sensation hit him like a mallet, so startling he heaved upright, spilling stew onto his buckskin shirt. He looked wildly around, then swore lustily.

"Will you cut it out? There's no one else here, simpleton! Keep this up and you're liable to burst your heart vessels and wind up like your uncle Hiram, as addlepated as a loon and always droolin' spittle out the corners of your mouth!"

Old Charlie finished his meal in relative peace. Twice the sensation plagued him, but each time he ignored it. There was only so much silliness a man could abide, and he'd reached his limit.

Propping his feet on the table, Old Charlie slipped a hand into his possibles bag, which hung over the back of the chair. He fished out his pipe and makings and tamped the pipe full. To light it he went to the fireplace and hunkered. As he sucked on the stem, inhaling smoke, the skittering noise was repeated. He ignored it too. The mouse, or whatever it was, could wait.

"If'n there's one thing I've learned over the years," Old Charlie said as he straightened, "it's that a man has to have his priorities in order."

Rather than return to the chair, Old Charlie sat down right where he was. At peace with himself and the world for the first time that day, he cheerfully puffed, blowing small circles of smoke into the air, a trick taught him by a Cheyenne.

It's too bad I don't have a son to teach the trick to, Old Charlie reflected, *or any grandchildren.* The lack always weighed heavily on his heart. He'd wanted children. Lord Almighty, how he'd wanted them! And he'd tried his best with Dove at Dawn and later Clay Pot. The latter gave him a daughter, the genuine apple of his eye, and he'd doted over that infant like she was the Queen of Sheba until that fateful day when a white man brought smallpox to the Mandan village and wiped out every last man, woman, and child.

The deaths of his wife and little girl had been almost more than Old Charlie could bear, and he'd gone off into the hills to kill himself. He'd found a nice hill with pretty flowers and a few aspens and had stuck the end of a pistol into his mouth and cocked the hammer. But he couldn't do it. He couldn't take his own life. It was his one cowardice, as he called it, and he never forgave himself for not having the courage to go join them, wherever they were.

From out of nowhere the eerie sensation hit him once more. Old Charlie snapped his head up. He happened to glance at the far corner where he kept his stock of ale, and he was positively stupefied to see a face just like the one he'd beheld that morning staring at him as brazenly as could be.

"I've had too much ale," Old Charlie said, and closed his eyes for a bit. When he opened them, the horrible apparition was still there, still staring with a sort of detached hostility, like a painter sizing up its prey.

Old Charlie tried to recollect if he had placed the plank back over the hole after he retrieved the ale, but couldn't. Either way, how had the creature gotten *into* the hole? There was no other way in or out except through the opening in the floor.

"What do you want?" Old Charlie demanded. Naturally, the creature didn't answer. Its slanted eyes were almost as red as the ones he'd seen in the cleft. It must be one of the same creatures, he concluded. The thing had followed him home and been spying on him all day, which accounted for his spooked spells.

"Go away, runt. You're nothin' but a miserable nuisance." Old Charlie wagged a hand at it, but the face might as well have been etched from stone. "I mean it," he warned. "I'm tired of being trifled with. Go pester someone else."

Thin lips curled, exposing tapered teeth in a hideous grin.

"Are you mockin' me, damn your hide?" Old Charlie swept to his feet so fast, he surprised himself. He hurled his pipe at the mocking visage but missed. Lightning quick, the creature dropped from view.

Old Charlie drew his pistol and dashed over, warily peeking over the edge. The hole was empty. No critter, no new hole on either side to show how it had got there, not a blessed thing. "I'm plumb crazy," he declared. It was the only explanation. The creature couldn't have been there. Not unless it could swim through solid earth.

Small prints at the bottom jarred him. Old Charlie's senses weren't deceiving him. He wasn't insane, either. The creature *was* under his cabin! Where had it gone? Kneeling, Old Charlie lowered his head partially into the hole. When he built the place, he'd deliberately left a two-inch gap between the planks and the ground. Barely enough room for a mouse, let alone one of those—*things*. Yet when he scanned the inky gap, he detected rustling to his right. Abruptly, crimson eyes blazed like burning coals.

"I'll be damned!"

The eyes rushed toward him. Old Charlie jerked upward, shoving the section of plank over the hole and slamming it down. A thump against the bottom lifted one end. "I'll show you!" Old Charlie fumed, drawing his flintlock. He fired into the center of the board, drilling a hole as big around as a man's thumb, slivers flying every which way.

Acrid smoke tingled Old Charlie's nose as he scrambled backward and hastily reloaded. His ears were ringing, and his heart pounded wildly. Fingers shaking, he opened his powder horn, taking several deep breaths to calm himself. "How dare they!" he roared. After he had been so friendly, too.

Loud scratching broke out under the floor. Not from the hole, but from almost directly under him! He jumped up and backpedaled, continuing to reload. The creature was trying to claw up through the boards! "No, you don't!" Snaking a ball from his ammo pouch, he hastily shoved it into the barrel with his thumb, then darted to the counter where he had left his ramrod. "I'll fix your mangy hide!"

The scratching grew louder when more sounds erupted from a different spot, close to the door.

"Two of you, eh?" Old Charlie said, shoving the ball in all the way. "Well, it won't make a difference! I've got plenty of ammo!" A tiny hole appeared where he had been sitting a second before, the tip of a sharp claw jutting out. *That plank is an inch thick!* he realized, stunned that anything could rip through it with such incredible swiftness. Striding over, he pointed the pistol at the hole.

The claw was yanked down, almost as if the creature knew what Old Charlie was about to do. He fired, the ball coring the hole and cracking the plank. He expected a screech, a yip of agony, something, but either he'd killed it outright or missed, because heavy silence greeted the blast.

Scratching resumed near the door. Old Charlie ran to his rifle, propped in a front corner. *He would blow the varmints to kingdom come!* He had to gauge where the second one was by the racket it was making, which stopped the moment he sighted down the barrel. He squeezed off the shot anyway.

A gust of cool wind fanned Old Charlie as he pivoted, seeking more evidence that the things were trying to get at him. "Where are you?" he raged. "Hiding?" He lifted the powder horn to pour black powder into the rifle, then had a thought that chilled the blood in his veins. *Where did that breeze come from? The door and the window are both closed.*

Or so Old Charlie assumed until he rotated and saw the shutter flung wide. On the counter stood one of the things, firelight highlighting its feral features. "Abomination!" he shouted. "Vile spawn of Satan!" His fingers flew as he sought to get off another shot.

The creature held an object of its own. Old Charlie blinked when he recognized what it was, then laughed. "You can't hurt me with that puny toy!"

He was wrong.

Outside, a raccoon that often visited the cabin for table scraps was crouched among the trees, afraid to approach any closer. It heard a twang and a thump, and afterward strident sobbing that ended eventually in a series of hair-raising screams. Terrified, the raccoon raced off into the night.

And so the nightmare began.

Chapter Two

It was cleaning day at the King cabin.

Eight-year-old Evelyn King loathed it, loathed it with a passion seldom seen in one so young. It was all work and no fun. Her mother insisted on washing everything that wasn't tied down: clothes, curtains, towels, even the bearskin rug. They dusted, they mopped, they polished, they oiled. In three days, when they were done, they'd have the cleanest cabin in the Rocky Mountains. And all for what? Evelyn repeatedly asked. Just so they could go and dirty the place up again. How silly. But that was how grown-ups did things. Backward.

"I wish a tree would fall on me," Evelyn remarked while trudging down a well-used trail, carrying a bucket.

"Why's that?" responded sixteen-year-old Louisa May Clark, her companion. Eyes as deep blue as the lake ahead regarded her with amusement.

"If I break my leg, maybe Ma will let me loaf and Zach and you can do all the work."

"You're fooling yourself. Loafing isn't in your mother's vocabulary."

21

David Thompson

"I reckon you're right. She'd probably have me polish the pots and pans, since I could do that sitting down." Evelyn sighed masterfully. "Cleaning house is the one thing I hate more than my brother."

"That's not true," Louisa said. "You care for Zach. I've seen it with my own eyes."

"When? That night I brought in firewood for him? It wasn't because I cared. He agreed to do my chores for the next two days."

They were quite a contrast, these two girls. Evelyn King was dark of complexion and hair, befitting her mixed lineage of white and Shoshone. A bundle of energy, she was always on the go, always getting into mischief. Louisa was taller and leaner, and much more deliberate in her speech and manner. The death of her father in the past year had added a layer of reserve to her usually quiet demeanor. They were opposites, these two, as opposite as two people could be, yet in the past several months they had grown to care for each other as deeply as two sisters.

Ironically, it was Lou who wore beaded buckskins, a gift from Winona King, Evelyn's mother. Shirt and pants were finely crafted, smooth and soft, the finest Lou ever owned. Evelyn King wore a green dress, also made by Winona, complete with ribbons and bows such as Winona had seen white women wear at Bent's Fort.

"Look at the bright side," Louisa commented. "By this time tomorrow we'll be done. No more housecleaning until next spring."

"Which will be here before we know it," Evelyn lamented. "If it were up to me, we'd clean only once a year. And only if the cabin needed it."

Lou thought of her own mother, who had died on the arduous trek west. She thought of how her ma had cleaned their house twice a week, rain or shine, summer and winter, year in and year out. She never had understood why her mother did it so often. The few times she'd inquired, her ma always said, "Because it has to be done." What kind of answer was that?

Mountain Nightmare

Going around a bend, Lou spotted a familiar figure down by the lake and her heart leaped in her breast. "Look! Zach's watering the horses!"

"So? Maybe he'll fall in and give us something to laugh about." Evelyn didn't share the older girl's enthusiasm for her brother. She'd just as soon he married Lou next week instead of next year like he was supposed to, and move out. Although she'd miss Louisa. It was nice having another girl to talk to, real nice.

"Oh, hush," Lou said, absently fluffing her hair and tugging on the hem of her buckskin shirt so it would cling to her admittedly underendowed chest. "He's not as bad as you make him out to be."

"Easy for you to say," Evelyn replied. "You're the one who goes around making cow eyes at him all the time."

"I do not."

"Then what? You open your eyes wider just to see him better?"

Lou wasn't going to argue with Zach so close. "You sure are a caution, you know that?" was her riposte as she strolled into the open and hooked her arms behind her slender back. "Howdy, handsome," she called out.

Zachary King had heard them coming from a long way off. He prided himself on having the ears of a bobcat, the eyes of an eagle. As should every Shoshone warrior. In keeping with Zach's preference for his mother's people over his father's, he had on buckskins much like Lou's and was armed with a long knife in a beaded sheath on his right hip. "Flower of my heart," he greeted Louisa in the Shoshone tongue, switching to English when his sister giggled. "It takes two of you to fetch a bucket of water?"

"Your pa didn't think it was safe for Evelyn to go alone," Lou said, "not with all the strange things that have been going on."

Zach knew what she meant. The strangeness had started about a moon earlier when the horses took to acting up most nights, nickering and stamping as if there were a mountain lion in the

23

corral. Every night he and his pa ran out with their Hawkens; every night they found nothing to explain it. Along about the same time, they started to hear occasional noises in the nearby forest, the patter of feet or paws and the occasional cracking of twigs. Again, he and his pa always investigated and never found a thing.

Then stuff around the cabin began to move of its own accord, or disappear. First was an ax, which his father had left embedded in the stump of a pine overnight. The next day it was found lying on the lake shore. Later, a saddle was dragged from the tack shed behind the corral and into the forest, where they found it in a clump of high weeds. An empty water skin and a coil of rope disappeared.

Zach's pa originally fretted that marauding hostiles were in the area, but as time passed and none of them was harmed and the hostiles never showed themselves, Nate King confessed to being as much in the dark as everyone else. Which shocked Zach more than the mystery. His father *always* had an answer. Nate was widely considered one of the savviest mountain men alive, ranked right up there with Shakespeare McNair, Jim Bridger, and Old Charlie Walker.

Now Zach rested a hand on the hilt of his knife and smirked. "Evelyn doesn't need to worry. Whatever's been nosing around our place wouldn't want a scruffy bundle of bones like her."

"Be nice," Lou said.

Evelyn bristled like a riled porcupine. "You have your gall, Stalking Coyote!" she snapped, using his Shoshone name. "If you were half the hunter you claim to be, you'd have tracked down whatever it is by now."

"Please be nice," Louisa stressed. It upset her, their constant spatting. Winona King claimed it was normal, but having never had a brother or sister of her own, Lou couldn't comprehend why they were forever at each other's throat.

A sharp retort was on the tip of Zach's tongue, but he held it in. Evelyn was blood kin, after all, even if he did have a daily urge to drop her off the handiest cliff. And, too, she had a point.

His prowess as a hunter was another ability he took pride in. Yet he hadn't been able to find so much as a clue as to the identity of the nightly prowler. Nor had his father, which was even more remarkable, for it was said among the Shoshones that Grizzly Killer, as his father was known, could track a flea across solid rock. An exaggeration, but not by much.

Louisa didn't like for anyone to upset her betrothed, even his own sister. "That's not fair," she said defending him. "Your pa said himself that in all his years, he's never seen the like. Trying to find whoever is to blame is like trying to find a ghost."

Zach saw a chance to change the subject. "There are no such things as ghosts," he flatly stated.

"Shows how much you know," Evelyn said. "Otter Tail saw one once, during the Blood Moon. As big as life it was, and all shimmery and scary."

"Otter Tail has been seeing and hearing things since a Blackfoot war club rattled his brainpan," Zach noted. "Remember those pink buffalo he saw? And the thunderbird?"

"My grandma claimed to have seen a ghost," Lou mentioned. "When she was no older than Evelyn. It floated into her bedroom and stared at her for a while, then smiled and floated off."

Had it been anyone else, Zach would have made a comment to the effect that her grandmother was as crazy as Otter Tail. But this was Louisa, the girl he loved, the one he was going to take for his wife. So he smiled sweetly and said instead, "As that may be, why would a ghost steal a rope? Or drag a saddle into the woods?"

Evelyn had a burst of inspiration. "Maybe it's a kid, like us! A real kid, not a ghost."

"Be serious."

"She could be right," Lou said. "Think about it. Dragging that saddle off and leaving the ax by the lake are things a kid would do, for a prank. Scaring the stock, the rope, it all fits."

Zach considered another aspect. "It would also explain why Pa and I can't find tracks. If it's a young kid, they wouldn't weigh much and wouldn't leave much sign." He looked at his sister. "You could be onto something, sprout."

"Let's tell Pa right away," Evelyn suggested, starting to turn.

"What's your hurry?" Zach snagged her arm. "Why bother him when he has enough on his mind? If it is a kid, we'll catch him ourselves."

"What makes you think it's a boy?" Lou said. "It could just as well be a girl."

Zach hadn't thought of that.

"The thing is," Louisa went on, "where did it come from? How did it get here? Your valley is so remote, so high up."

"A few days' ride to the north is South Pass and the route to the Oregon country," Zach reminded her. "Scores of wagons pass along it every month in the summer. Maybe a white kid strayed from camp, became lost, and wandered down here."

Even Evelyn saw the flaw in his reasoning. "Then why don't they show themselves? Pa and Lou are white. What do they have to be afeared of?"

Zach shrugged. "Who knows? White people do strange things." He winked at Lou to take the sting out of his remark. "Or maybe it's an Indian, someone whose parents were made outcasts." The odds were slim in either case, but they were the only possibilities he could think of.

Evelyn giggled. She liked the idea of snaring the culprit by themselves. It was exciting, an adventure all their own, a welcome break in the boredom of cabin cleaning. "How will we go about it? What do we do?"

"Since we can't track this kid down, we'll have to make him, or her, come to us," Zach proposed.

"How do we do that?" Evelyn asked.

"Simple. We do what every hunter does when an animal is too elusive to find. Or what Pa does to lure beaver into his traps. We'll set out some bait."

Evelyn liked their adventure more and more by the second. "Set out something the kid can't resist, you mean? Like honey, maybe? Or a plate of Ma's sweetcakes?"

"Something like that," Zach said, warming to the enterprise too. Capturing the elusive prankster would be a challenge, and he loved challenges. Besides, his father would be tremendously impressed if he succeeded where his pa had failed.

"Just so we agree on one thing," Lou commented. "We don't harm this kid. He's lost and scared and needs our help. So no deadfalls, or pits with stakes at the bottom. Fair enough?"

Zach couldn't help feeling that she was taking some of the fun out of it, but he had to admit he would make his folks extremely mad if he squashed some little kid with a log rigged to drop on their noggin. "All right. We'll start tonight, after supper."

Just then, from up the trail to the cabin, a deep voice boomed. "How long does it take to fill a bucket?"

"Uh-oh," Evelyn said. "Pa's coming."

Nate King was a big, brawny man, as rugged as the land he called home. His buckskins and moccasins were typical of a full-blooded Shoshone—or a white man with a Shoshone wife, a man who had been formally adopted into the tribe. His shoulder-length black hair, unlike his son's, wasn't braided in the Shoshone fashion, but an eagle feather did jut from the back of his head. Crisscrossing his broad chest were his powder horn and ammo pouch, while under his left arm hung his possibles bag. He never went anywhere without them. Nor did he go beyond the clearing in which his cabin sat without taking his heavy Hawken and a brace of matched smoothbore flintlock pistols. As if that were not enough, also wedged under his wide brown leather belt was a tomahawk, and on his left hip in a beaded sheath hung a long-bladed knife with an antler hilt.

Nate King's eyes were as green as the lush vegetation flanking the trail. They alertly roved over the undergrowth, questing for clues, for spoor that would give him a clue to the identity of their recent visitor.

Nate hadn't said anything to the others, but he was worried. So far the visits had been harmless, if annoying. But what if that changed? What worried him most was that for once in his life, he was powerless to protect his loved ones. Try as he might, he couldn't track their visitor down. He knew as little now as he had that morning the ax was taken, which had been a harbinger of things to come.

Well, Nate mused, *that isn't entirely true.* He did know a little more. When the saddle was dragged off, he'd found what appeared to be a partial print in a patch of bare earth. Only thing was, the heel print, if that is what it had been, was so small that it couldn't belong to whoever took it. No one that size could move his saddle, let alone drag it a hundred yards.

Then there were the claws. Several times now, near the cabin, Nate had come on faint, tiny marks that reminded him of a cat's claws. Which would lead to the conclusion that whatever was bedeviling them was a wild beast. Yet what wild animal would swipe an ax? Or a rope or old water skin?

Nate shook his head to dispel the troubling questions. He was becoming obsessed with the mystery. Maybe he should forget about it for a while and tackle the problem afresh later. Emerging onto the lake shore, he grinned at the sight of his youngest hauling the bucket from the lake and spilling water all over the front of her dress. "Your mother thought you might have drowned."

"Ah, Pa," Evelyn said, grunting. "It weighs a ton."

"Sorry we've taken so long, Mr. King," Louisa said. "We got to chatting and didn't realize."

Nate glanced at his oldest, whose cheeks tinged red, and almost laughed. The two lovebirds were like two halves of the same coin. They couldn't stand to be apart, and were forever contriving excuses to go off alone. He remembered being the same way once. Young love was romantic love, and could no more be held in check than the tide or the waxing and waning of the moon. "I needed to stretch my legs anyway," he said.

"We were talking about whoever's been playing tricks on us," Evelyn said, receiving a sharp glance from her brother. She shot him one right back. *How dumb does he think I am?* She wasn't going to tell what they were up to.

"Oh." Nate frowned. So much for forgetting about the mystery for a while. "And what did you decide?"

Zach answered before the others could. "We're as stumped as you are."

Evelyn said jokingly, "Maybe it was that little man I saw a while back." To her astonishment, her father spun toward her as if he were fixing to pounce.

"What little man?"

Zach chuckled. "Don't listen to her, Pa. She's being childish, like always." He elaborated. "A couple of weeks ago she told us that she'd seen a shriveled old man in a pit, and she wanted us to go have a look-see. It was a story she made up to make us look foolish."

"I did not make it up!" Evelyn stomped a foot. "He was there, I tell you! In a cave in the ground, not a pit! He was all brown and dried up, like a berry that's been in the hot sun too long."

Nate tended to agree with his son. The story was ridiculous. But then there was that heel print he'd discovered. And his daughter was so sincere. Resting a callused hand on her shoulder, he asked, "Why didn't you let your mother or me know?"

"I figured you'd laugh at me, like Zach did," Evelyn said, which was only partly true. There had been something about the little man, something she couldn't describe, that had scared her so terribly she didn't want to go back.

"You know better, sweet one," Nate said, gently squeezing. "So long as you always tell us the truth, we'll never doubt your word. Not ever." He gazed skyward. They had five or six hours of daylight left, more than enough. "Take me there."

"Right this minute?" Evelyn said, troubled by the request yet at the same time overjoyed to get out of doing more work. "What about the water Ma needs?"

"Lou and Zach will take it back up, with the horses." Nate clasped his daughter's hand. "Let's go. Is it far?"

"Not at all." Evelyn smirked at Zach and guided her father toward the north tree line. She had nothing to fear with him along.

David Thompson

Her father could handle anything. Why, before she was born, he'd slain a grizzly with just a hunting knife!

Zach and Louisa watched the pair enter the forest. "Did you see how your father acted?" she inquired. "Like he was stuck with a pin?"

"I saw. You'd almost think those old legends were true."

It had been quite a while since Nate and Evelyn King had enjoyed a leisurely stroll in the wild. So long, the father regretted not doing so regularly. A velvet blue sky was decorated by fluffy clouds, and a soft breeze from the northwest provided a bit of relief from the late-summer heat.

Insects buzzed, butterflies flitted from flower to flower, and high on the air currents a pair of golden eagles soared. All in all, it was the kind of day Nate appreciated most. The kind that made him glad to be alive, and reminded him of why he had taken to living in the Rockies instead of in New York City, where he was born.

Roseate shafts of sunlight penetrated the foliage, gleaming like precious yellow ore. In the higher terrace a gray squirrel scampered. A grazing doe and fawn inspected the intruders, then gracefully bounded off, tails erect.

Evelyn wasn't in any mood to admire the beautiful scenery. As confident as she was her pa could protect her, she couldn't shake the nagging unease that had afflicted her when she stumbled on the withered little man. It was similar to the heart-stopping fear she'd experienced when she was exploring the south shore of the lake last year and happened on a snake den, a wide crack filled with hundreds of writhing serpents, rattlers and others, all roiling and hissing. Petrified, she had thrown back her head and screamed, screamed, screamed, probably scaring the snakes as much as they scared her. Luckily, her mother had rushed to her rescue, pulled her to safety, and calmed her down.

Ever since, Evelyn hadn't much liked anything that wriggled and squirmed.

Now, studying the landscape, she tried to recall exactly where

30

the little man had been. She hadn't been paying much attention that day, just wandering here and there, dallying. There had been a dead tree close by. And a knoll to the northeast, a knoll with a large, flat boulder at the top.

"So," Nate said to break the quiet, "what do you think about your brother and Louisa getting married?"

"I sort of feel sorry for her."

"Your brother is a fine young man. He'll work hard to be a good husband. She could do a lot worse, princess."

"Will they squabble like he and I do, Pa?"

"Sometimes married couples fight a lot, sometimes they don't. It depends on the couple. The important thing is that they learn to work their problems out, that they always kiss and make up, as people like to say."

"I'd rather kiss a toad than Zach."

Nate snickered. "When you're older, you'll understand."

"Ma and you sure do say that a lot. But if kissing boys is part of growing up, I'd rather stay just as I am my whole life long."

Children said the darnedest things, Nate reflected. Then again, childhood was *supposed* to be a time of innocence, of blissful ignorance of the harsh realities of the world. Let Evelyn have her flights of fancy. All too soon, she would grow up. All too soon, she would taste the bitter pills every person swallowed on the perilous road from the cradle to the grave.

"So where's this cave of yours?" Nate asked, hiding his doubt. He had been over practically every square foot of their valley, and never in all his meandering had he seen any sign of one.

"It shouldn't take long," Evelyn said, secretly worried she wouldn't find the landmarks. He wouldn't believe her, and she'd be a laughingstock to her brother.

"This close to the lake?" Nate said, his doubt rising. Were it at the base of the ring of peaks surmounting their valley, he would be more inclined to accept her account.

Evelyn bobbed her oval chin. "It surprised me, too, Pa. I was searching for some of those blue flowers Ma named me after." Like her brother, Evelyn had a Shoshone name, which, translated into English, became Blue Flower. "I went around a tree and there was a hole in the ground, a pit that had never been there before."

"You said it was a cave."

"Well, it might have been. I mean, it looked like one. As if the roof had fallen in. And at the bottom was the shriveled little man. You should have seen his face, Pa. It gave me goose bumps." Evelyn suddenly clapped her hands and squealed. "There! There's the dead tree!"

Hurrying around it, Evelyn spotted the knoll with the flat boulder. "This is the place!" She swiveled to the left, to where the hole should be—only, the ground was unbroken, the surface littered with fallen pine needles and dead leaves.

"Here?" Nate said, moving a few strides past her. "Are you sure?"

"God's honest truth, Pa," Evelyn said earnestly. She couldn't understand it. She just couldn't. "I was standing right about where you are. The pit was right in front of me."

"It's not here now," Nate said, stating the obvious. And equally obvious, it never had been, nor had there been a wrinkled old man. It had all been in her head. Her childish imagination had gotten the better of her. He must inform Winona so she could sit Evelyn down and have a long talk about the difference between reality and make-believe.

Evelyn's eyes moistened. "I don't know what to say, Pa. It's gone. Someone must have filled in the hole."

Doesn't she see how silly that is? Nate mused. Turning, he sadly smiled and patted her back. "Don't let it bother you. We all make mistakes."

"You don't believe me, do you?"

Nate King could have lied. He could have told her he did. But it went against every personal value he held dear. From the time his children could toddle, he'd taught them to always tell the truth. Taught them that lying was evil. That it was a nasty habit, a refuge of the vile, the weak, the confused. Speaking with two tongues, as the Shoshones phrased it, was despicable, something no King would ever do. So now, confronted by his own ideal, he practiced what he preached.

"I believe you *think* you saw a little man. But he wasn't really there."

They departed, the father tenderly holding his daughter's hand, the girl softly weeping.

Chapter Three

Touch the Clouds was a legend among the Shoshones. Rightfully so. In the entire history of his people no warrior had counted more coup. No warrior had stolen more horses. His prowess in combat was extraordinary, befitting someone of his gigantic stature. Over seven feet tall, weighing in excess of two hundred and fifty pounds, Touch the Clouds was a solid mass of muscle, melded to a keen mind.

On this sunlit day the Shoshone legend was on his way back to his village after a dozen sleeps spent hunting in a high valley nestled among pristine, snow-crowned peaks. On four packhorses were the results of his labor, enough elk meat to last his family for moons to come. Ever prudent, Touch the Clouds planned to dry and salt the meat to be ready for the upcoming winter. All the signs hinted it would be long and hard.

Prominent among those signs were the long-necked geese. For some time now, the big warrior had seen V-shaped flocks winging southward—much earlier than usual. The Hunting Moon had begun, yes, but the Falling Leaf Moon was many sleeps off yet. For

David Thompson

the geese to be traveling so early must mean the moons ahead would be cold, and heavy with snow.

Touch the Clouds was alone. Usually warriors traveled in pairs when far afield for mutual protection, but the mighty Shoshone had no need of someone to watch his back. He was supremely confident in his ability to prevail over any and all threats, man or beast. Hadn't he bested the Blackfeet, the Piegans, the devious Sioux? Hadn't he had slain silvertips with nothing but his lance, or in one instance his seventy-five-pound pull ash bow? Only the famed Grizzly Killer had killed more.

Now the lance was in Touch the Cloud's left hand, a broad shield strapped to his left wrist. His bow and a quiver bulging with arrows were slung across his back. Intricate beadwork decorated his buckskins, and his raven hair hung in thick braids.

As the Shoshone neared a squat structure close to a bubbling stream, his dark eyes narrowed. The wooden lodge was the home of Charles Walker, or Talks to Himself, as the Shoshones called the oldster. It had been three—no, four—winters since Touch the Clouds saw the wizened white-eye last. They'd shared a pot of coffee and swapped tales of the days before the beaver trade, when the number of white men in the mountains could be counted on one hand.

Touch the Clouds liked the old man, which was more than he could say about most whites. Those like Walker and Nate King, those who had learned to adapt and lived much as the Indian did, Touch the Clouds respected highly. The others, the greedy ones who were interested only in filling their pockets with jingling metal coins, and those who looked down their noses at the red man on general principle, Touch the Clouds avoided.

The big warrior's knowledge of the white man's tongue was scanty. He simply hadn't bothered to learn it. The strange chirping hurt his throat, which was why it always amazed him that his cousin, Winona, Nate King's wife, had been able to master it so completely.

Straightening, Touch the Clouds called out in Shoshone, "Talks to Himself, you have a visitor."

36

Ordinarily, that was all it would take to bring the oldster from his nook, all smiles and nonstop words. But the door stayed shut. Nor did the mule appear at the corner of the corral, as was its wont.

Touch the Clouds noticed other things. The ground in front of the cabin had not been trod on in some time; no fresh tracks were visible. The acrid scent of wood smoke wasn't hanging in the air, as it usually did. And across the top of the door was a recently woven spiderweb.

Dismounting, Touch the Clouds let the reins dangle. He adjusted his heavy shield and transferred the lance to his right hand. Then, hefting it, he cautiously moved forward, aware that the customary sounds of wildlife were absent. Something was wrong here, drastically wrong.

Touch the Clouds was close enough to see the spider in the center of the gossamer webbing when he also spied a symbol painted low on the door, at knee level. Painted in red, it wasn't like any symbol Touch the Clouds had ever seen, yet he felt he should know what it was.

Few whites were aware of the fact, but among many tribes were skilled artists whose paintings and rock carvings were left for posterity to enjoy. Nate King, Touch the Clouds remembered, had been surprised to learn how many rock paintings there were in Shoshone territory, and even more surprised when Touch the Clouds told him that some of the paintings had been made by the Old Ones, those who lived there before the coming of the Shoshones.

Studying the symbol on the door, Touch the Clouds suddenly realized where he knew it from. A long time before, he had visited an area where smoking waters shot out of the ground high into the air. In the vicinity were spires of stone adorned with symbols reputed to have been left by the Old Ones. One of the symbols he had seen was exactly like the one on the door. He was sure of it. It depicted what he took to be a tiny arrow above a prone body, and below both was a straight horizontal line over three small dots.

Touch the Clouds had no idea what it meant. The straight line and the three dots were similar to the Shoshone symbol for fear, which consisted of a straight line and two dots drawn in the chest of a sketched figure, which in turn stood for the person who was afraid.

Buzzing drew the warrior's gaze to the open window. Flies were entering and leaving in droves. An odor assailed his nostrils, an odor every battled-seasoned warrior had smelled at one time or another, and Touch the Clouds scowled. It did not bode well for Talks to Himself.

Touch the Clouds gingerly tried the wooden latch and shoved. The door squeaked inward on leather hinges. A foul stench gushed out, assaulting him, and the Shoshone took a breath and held it as he boldly stepped inside.

The flies were thicker indoors, milling by the hundreds, drawn from leagues around by some instinct only they had. They covered the counter, they covered the table, they droned over dried puddles on the floor. An agitated swarm rose from a disjointed shape that lay in the rectangle of sunlight admitted by the doorway.

Bitter bile rose in Touch the Clouds' throat, and he swallowed it down. He was no squeamish child to be made sick by the sight of death, grisly as it might be. And this was one of the grisliest ever.

Old Charlie Walker, or what was left of him, could be identified by stringy wisps of gray hair and the quartz necklace he'd always worn, a gift from his second wife, Clay Pot. His clothes were in tatters, shredded as if by knives. His flesh—that is, the parts of him not devoured down to the bone—bore countless small bite marks.

Touch the Clouds surveyed the interior. The table and chair had been upended. A cooking pot lay on its side, clumps of rotting stew beside it. Clothing, blankets, and tools had been wildly scattered, the clothes torn, the blankets ripped, the implements bent or broken. Whoever had killed Talks to Himself had gone on a spree of utter destruction, reveling in the ruin.

Whoever? The Shoshone looked at the remains again. Surely, he must be mistaken. Surely, this was not the work of a man but the result of an attack by a wild beast. Talks to Himself had been *eaten*. Yet it was difficult to reconcile. Mountain lions and wolverines wouldn't bother to wreak havoc; they would eat and go. A grizzly might indulge in mayhem, but Charlie Walker had intentionally built the door and window much too narrow for a silvertip to fit through.

What else could have done it? Touch the Clouds wondered as he checked for spoor. Blood had been spattered on the walls, on the ceiling, on the floor. Whatever was responsible couldn't possibly avoid stepping in it. Yet try as he might, Touch the Clouds couldn't find any tracks until he examined the counter under the window, and then those he did find only added to the riddle.

Something had left a pair of small prints. In general shape they were like those of a bear's, and were capped by claws, as a bear's would be. Judging by telltale streaks that bordered them, both feet had been quite hairy. Another bear trait.

But Touch the Clouds wasn't deceived. A bear wasn't to blame. He noticed claw marks on the edge of the window, and leaning out, saw smudges on the ground where the creature had jumped down. Going out and inspecting the soil, he learned there had been two, or more, and that they had gone off to the south, leaving red smears in the grass. They must have been coated with blood.

Touch the Clouds tracked them through a belt of woodland, across a meadow, to the entrance to a narrow ravine. Here he halted. The same inner guide that had preserved his life in scores of battles now warned him not to go any farther.

The Shoshone had a decision to make. He'd liked Walker, true, but it wasn't his place to avenge the white man. Or lose his life trying to. Whatever had happened didn't concern him. He should ride on and forget it.

Retracing his steps, Touch the Clouds thought about the symbol on the door. About the consumed flesh and the footprints. An incredible connection occurred to him, one he would never credit if he hadn't seen the aftermath with his own eyes. One only a Shoshone would fully appreciate.

The symbol demanded investigation. Squatting, Touch the Clouds memorized it, the exact placement of the arrow and the figure and the line, searing it indelibly in his memory so when he reached his village he could consult the elders. That done, he entered. Enough firewood was on hand for his purpose. He built four equal-size piles at various points, then opened his pouch and removed his fire steel and flint.

A twinge of guilt racked him. Burning Walker's possessions wasn't right, but Touch the Clouds dared not let another white man happen on the cabin. While it was doubtful Indians would be blamed, it might add to the bad blood that already existed. The astounding truth, if his deduction was right, and if it was to become widely known, would draw whites from all over. They would have to see for themselves. And more would die.

The cabin ignited rapidly. Flames slithered to the walls, then licked higher, engulfing the dwelling. Touch the Clouds backed out and watched dark clouds of smoke billow skyward. The pyre could be seen for miles, but it couldn't be helped. All evidence must be destroyed.

The Old Ones are back. The thought was so stupefying that Touch the Clouds needed time to let the full import sink in. Climbing onto his mount, he kneed it to the northeast, toward his village. He had been debating whether to pay his cousin a visit. It was always good to see Winona and Grizzly Killer. But this was more important. The elders must be informed, a course of action formulated.

Winona and her family could wait.

The giant warrior reined up on a ridge and shifted. Fire consumed the cabin from bottom to top, devouring it just as its owner had been devoured. Soon there would be no trace of either save for charred embers and bones. Satisfied, Touch the Clouds rode on.

The secret of the symbol was safe with him.

* * *

Mountain Nightmare

Winona King loved to clean. She loved to have the cabin neat and tidy, just as her mother had loved to keep their lodge spotless. "How a woman keeps her home is a measure of her character," Winona's mother had instructed Winona when she twelve. "Your aunt, Tall Willow, keeps her lodge clean of dust and dirt, just as she always wears clean dresses and keeps her hair brushed. Compare her to Crooked Ear, who leaves dirty pans lying around, and who washes her blankets but once a moon. Her dresses are as dirty as her pans, her hair as greasy as bear fat."

Winona's mother had another point to make. "A woman's lodge mirrors how she feels about her family. What woman would want her loved ones to live in filth? Show how much you care for yours by making the extra effort to keep your lodge clean. I know many women complain. They say cleaning is drudgery. And it is, if you do so with bitterness in your heart. Always remember you do it for those you love and you will never have cause to be bitter."

At the time, Winona had listened with half an ear. Lodge chores always bored her. She'd disliked being made to take clothes to a stream or having to beat a bearskin robe when she would much rather be playing with her friends. Only much later, after she had wed Grizzly Killer and had a home of her own, had the wisdom of her mother's advice sunk in.

Still, Winona made concessions. Where her mother had cleaned their lodge every day, she gave the cabin a light cleaning whenever it needed it. Twice a year, after the winter storms ended and again before the leaves started to fall, she gave her home a thorough going-over. The scrubbing and the scraping and the polishing were still tedious, but she did it without complaint because she did it out of love.

On this day, however, her affection was being put to the test. No one was cooperating. Her daughter carped constantly. Her prospective daughter-in-law was too tactful to complain but too much in love, and she kept daydreaming when she should be working. Her husband was preoccupied and had to be told everything twice. Which left her son, who made no secret of the con-

41

tempt he held for work he deemed beneath a warrior's dignity.

By the middle of the afternoon Winona had tolerated as much of this as she was willing to. Standing just outside the front door, she tiredly swatted at wisps of hair hanging over her sweating face. The cabin was almost clean, but she was a mess. Her everyday buckskin dress was caked with grime, her forearms were splotched with dirt, and her moccasins needed a dip in the lake. It never ceased to surprise her how dirty a cabin could get in only three or four moons. She puffed at her bangs and cupped a hand to her mouth to shout, then promptly lowered it.

Coming up the trail were Zach and Louisa May. He was leading the horses; she was toting the bucket. Of Evelyn there was no sign.

"Where's your sister?"

Zach had been hoping to stop under a large oak that bordered the clearing and steal a kiss from his bride-to be. Sometimes it seemed as if he couldn't get enough of her, of her soft lips and her warm hands, her twinkling eyes and playful grin. A year before, if anyone had said a girl would claim his heart before he saw eighteen winters, he'd have laughed in their face. But here he was, in love and glad of it. With a white girl, no less. When his Shoshone friends heard, they would tease him mercilessly. Or try to. "She led Pa off on a wild-goose chase. They won't be long."

"A wild-goose chase?" Winona repeated. Another of the white man's many colorful phrases that had no Shoshone equivalent. Listing them all would require a book the size of her husband's prized dictionary.

"Pa will tell you all about it, I expect," Zach said. He would never admit as much, but he didn't go into detail because it was bound to get his sister into trouble. Their mother was much stricter than their father, especially when it came to Evelyn's antics. Clucking to the horses, he guided them toward the corral gate.

Lou held out the bucket. "Where do you want this?"

Beckoning, Winona went inside. The heat was stifling even

with both windows open. Windows that boasted the only glass panes between the Muddy River and the Great Water. They were Winona's pride and joy. Glass was a rarity, the luxury of luxuries, and her secret to needing to houseclean only twice a year. She doted over her windows as she had heard white women doted over fine china.

Louisa carried the bucket to the counter. "Mrs. King, I'd like to learn more about some of the old Shoshone legends, if you don't mind."

About to go to work with a mop, Winona glanced up. "Which ones?"

"Any and all of them. Zach's told me a little. And since he's part Shoshone, I reckon I should learn all I can about your people."

The girl was so sweet. Winona had liked Louisa from the very beginning, even if she had been dubious that day Stalking Coyote brought Lou home and announced out of the blue that she was to be his mate. Winona had figured youthful infatuation was to blame, but they'd proven her wrong. They genuinely cared for each other. "My people have many legends, many stories about the early times. Coyote, the trickster, the father of the Shoshones, started our tribe when he married a woman whose favorite food was other people, and they had children who—"

"Wait a minute. Your people believe they're descended from a cannibal?" Lou giggled. "That's silly!"

"Is it? The Digger Shoshones and the Paiutes say that a tribe of red-headed cannibals once lived in the pine nut country. They were the terror of the land. At night they would steal into lodges and carry victims off. But one day the Paiutes had had enough and waged war on the cannibals, killing every last one."

"And you believe this tale?" Early on, Lou had been greatly impressed by her soon-to-be mother-in-law's intellect. Winona was one of the smartest women Lou had ever met. It showed in Winona's mastery of English, in her conversation, in a thousand and one little things. Next to Lou's own mother, Louisa had never thought as highly of any woman as she did Winona King. So to hear Winona say she believed red-headed cannibals once roamed the land surprised Lou immensely.

"Before my people claimed this territory," Winona went on, "it was the home to giants, and to beasts twice as big as buffalo, with teeth as long as your arm. Thunderbirds often swooped down and took babies and young children."

"Thunderbirds?" Lou recalled Zach mentioning that name once. Or had it been Evelyn?

"Great eagles, is how the whites would describe them. They had wings as wide as our cabin."

Lou couldn't resist laughing. "I'm sorry."

Winona was patient with her. "Maybe now you can understand how my people feel about white beliefs. The Garden of Eden. The serpent. The flood and Noah. To them, it is just as strange as their beliefs are to you." Winona paused, then went to a shelf on the west wall laden with books her husband had collected. She held up their Bible. "Do you believe in the white man's Scripture?"

"Of course," Louisa answered, adding, "Mind you, I haven't read it from beginning to end yet. But my ma used to read parts every night before she tucked me in."

"We also read every evening," Winona said. It was one of her favorite pastimes. She had learned a great deal about white culture, and about the world in general, from their little library.

In this regard the white man had an edge over the Indian, Winona belived. Her people passed on their traditions and knowledge by word of mouth and a few paintings and carvings. The whites, in contrast, had their whole history written down in complete detail. All the knowledge of the centuries was at their fingertips, knowledge they could use and improve on. To her way of thinking, it explained why the whites had invented so much more than her people. Firearms, compasses, magnifying glasses, carriages, they were all a direct result of the white man's vast store of facts and wisdom.

"I like the Twenty-third Psalm best," Lou said.

"So does my husband," Winona said. "But the thing that interests me most is that the Bible confirms much of what my people believe." She quoted from Genesis, chapter six, verse four. "There were giants in the earth in those days."

"I'd forgotten that," Lou admitted.

'I have often wondered what they mean by 'in the earth,' " Winona said. "Did the giants live underground?"

"Is that important?"

"According to our legends, the giants always lived in caves, and when they were attacked, they would retreat deep under the ground. My grandfather told me that when he was a boy, his father took him to a cavern where some giants sat, wrapped in old blankets. They were dead, and when my grandfather touched one, the blanket fell to pieces."

"You believed him?"

"My grandfather never told a lie in his life," Winona declared. "He also said the mountains are riddled with caves few know about. Like a honeycomb, he described it. To the south, about a week's ride, is one that extends down into the center of the earth." She replaced the Bible. "The creatures that dwell in them are not meant to be seen by human eyes."

To Lou it sounded like so much superstition. "All people have their monsters," she commented.

"Ours live mainly in lakes. To us, the giants are not much different than ordinary people. Just a lot bigger."

"What was that about lakes?"

"In some of the deeper ones live animals that can eat a man in three bites. Usually they stay at the bottom. But from time to time, when a canoe passes overhead, they rise to the surface, upend it, and feast." Winona dipped the mop into the bucket. "It's common for warriors to toss a dead deer into a lake before crossing to appease them."

"Don't your people have legends about little people, too?" Evelyn couldn't recollect what they were called.

"The NunumBi, yes. At one time they lived in great numbers. But they were driven into the far corners of the mountains, where they still exist, some say. They were vicious, those little ones.

45

They killed for the sake of killing. And they were very hard to slay.''

"How did your people drive them off, then?''

Winona began to swish the mop across the floor. "A buhagant, a Shoshone prophet, or what the whites would call a medicine man, discovered their great weakness. They cannot stand bright light. A torch thrust in front of their face will blind them, put them in a panic. Which is why they mainly come out at night.'' Swiping at a spot of dirt, she idly amended, "Or in the early morning and evening. But there have been no reports of NunumBi in many winters.''

"So you don't think Evelyn saw one?''

"She claims she did?'' Winona stopped mopping just as footsteps thudded outside and Zach appeared in the doorway.

"Ma! Come quick!''

They hastened out on his heels, around the cabin to the corral, and around the corral to the tack shed. Their saddles, normally stored on special pine racks, lay on the ground, covered with rents and holes. Most of their bridles were in bits and pieces.

"Look at what they did!'' Zach was furious at the wanton destruction. "I can't say exactly when. Everything was fine when I hung a bridle up last night. And I didn't think to look in here before I took the horses to water today, or I'd have noticed sooner.''

Crestfallen, Winona stooped and set one of the saddles on a rack. It could be repaired, but it would take a week or more. The bridles were beyond mending and needed to be replaced, another time-consuming task at a time when she had her hands full cleaning. "Who would do such a thing?''

Zach was more confident than ever it had to be a kid. No Indian would waste so much good tack. Steal it, yes, but not tear it apart.

"Clean up the mess, if you please,'' Winona said. "I'll tell your father when he gets back.'' Shaking her head in dismay, she walked off.

"Tonight's the night,'' Zach said when his mother was out of earshot. "I'm setting some traps before I turn in.'' He angrily kicked the ground. "Look at all this work they've cost us! Do you still want me to go easy on them? At least let me rig it so the kid breaks a leg."

Louisa was examining a bridle. "Do what you feel you have to."

"Really?" Zach had expected her to object.

"I don't think a person is to blame," Lou said, extending the bridle for him to inspect. "See for yourself. A knife wasn't used to cut this."

"What was?" Zach asked, taking it.

"Teeth."

Chapter Four

Supper was usually cheerful at the King homestead. The family talked about events of the day. They joked and laughed. The love they shared, the deep bond they had forged, shone like a beacon.

But not this particular evening. A somber air reigned. Nate picked at his food, worried more than ever now that their mysterious prowler had turned vicious. Winona was concerned for her daughter, who was so upset she wouldn't talk unless addressed. Zach was mulling how many traps he should set, and what kind. Louisa fretted that whatever had chewed the tack to ribbons might try to do the same to her betrothed. Evelyn was mired in a quicksand of self-doubt, brought on by not being able to trust her own senses.

They ate late. Nate and Zach had spent hours seeking sign, hoping to backtrack the culprit, to no avail. They had also brought the saddles and what little tack wasn't damaged into the cabin, piling it next to the bookshelf.

Spearing a piece of venison with his fork, Nate took a bite, then announced, "Tomorrow Zach and I are taking the tack shed

49

apart and rebuilding it at the front of the corral, where we can keep a better eye on it.''

''We are?'' Zach said. He'd rather have spent every waking moment searching for their elusive visitor.

''Is there something else you'd rather do?'' Nate asked, a bit irritably. His son wasn't fond of hard work unless it was work related to the hunt or counting coup.

Zach recognized his father's tone. ''Whatever you want is fine by me, Pa. But I don't know if moving the shed will help much. Next time, it could be the cabin they hit.''

Across the table, Evelyn, nipping at a boiled root, roused herself to say, ''Do you think whatever tore our saddles up will try and sneak into the cabin to do the same to our personal stuff?''

''Could be,'' Zach said.

Winona wished her son were as tactful as his father. ''Don't worry, Blue Flower. The shed door doesn't latch, like the cabin door does. Breaking in here would be harder.''

''A bear can work a latch if it tries,'' Zach noted. ''And whatever this animal is, it's as smart as any bear.''

''So far it's been lucky,'' Nate remarked. ''Sooner or later, the thing will slip up and leave sign for us to follow.'' He lifted his glass and swallowed some water. ''Shakespeare is due to stop by in a week or so. If we haven't caught it by then, he and I will go out and won't rest until we find it.''

What with everything that had occurred of late, Winona had forgotten about the impending visit of her husband's mentor. Shakespeare McNair had taken Nate under his wing when her husband first came to the mountains and taught the then young and brash greenhorn the essential skills Nate needed to survive and thrive. McNair's Flathead wife, Blue Water Woman, was one of her best friends. ''It will be marvelous to see them again.''

The news caused Zach to reconsider his plans. Instead of one or two traps, he'd better rig four or five. He had to catch the culprit before McNair arrived, or he could forget impressing his father. Shakespeare was the one person who knew more about tracking and hunting than his pa. Some said Shakespeare was the best alive. "Can I be excused?"

Winona nodded at his plate. "You haven't eaten much."

"I'm not very hungry." Which was true. Zach was too excited to give much thought to food. He pushed back the chair, went to the southwest corner, where his bedding and weapons were stored, and armed himself with a pair of pistols and his rifle.

"Where do you think you're going?" Winona demanded. His flair for getting into dangerous situations brought her no end of anxiety.

"Lou and I are going for a walk, like always," Zach fibbed, then glanced at his father. "We won't go far. I promise."

"Be sure you don't," Nate said. "The sun set half an hour ago. It'll be fully dark soon, and I want you inside by then."

"We'll keep our eyes skinned," Zach promised. Grasping his fiancée's hand, he hustled her out before his parents changed their minds, making straight for the tack shed. Twilight shrouded the valley, and a smattering of stars had blossomed. Down on the lake ducks were quacking, geeze honking, all part of their evening feeding ritual. An early owl voiced the eternal query of its kind.

Lou had a pistol of her own, under her belt, and she never took her free hand off it. "I don't like this," she commented.

"Don't tell me you're afraid," Zach said. Not as close as they were to the cabin, and with him there to watch over her. It disturbed him. If she was scared now, how would she react after they were man and wife and he went on a buffalo surround? Or on a raid with a Shoshone war party? Flinging the shed door inward, he gauged the width of the doorway, then hurried into the forest. The gloom darkened. Shadows clung to the bottoms of the trees, reaching out with inky claws.

Louisa shivered, and not from the temperature. She couldn't help herself. Her intuition screamed an alarm in her brain, railing at her to turn around, to get out of there and go back indoors. But she'd noticed how Zach looked at her a moment earlier, and she refused to appear cowardly in his eyes. "What are we after?" she whispered.

51

"A couple of long, fairly straight branches. And a log." Zach drew his knife and halted beside a stand of saplings. "Two of these should do." Honed steel made short shrift of the job. After trimming them, he handed the poles to her.

The log proved harder to find. Based on the width of the doorway, it couldn't be any wider than his shoulders, and it had to be heavy. But not so heavy that Zach couldn't lift it over his head. The first he spied was rife with rot. The second was too light. Not ten feet from it, though, was one that promised to work perfectly.

To set the trap required some ingenuity. Standing in the shed with the door almost shut, Zach hiked the log above it and held the log steady while Lou wedged the two poles against the bottom, one at either end. It was the same principle as a trip snare. Now, when the door was opened all the way, it would strike the poles, jarring them loose, and bring the log crashing down on the head of whoever or whatever entered.

"Crude, but it should work," Zach said.

They exited carefully, Zach pulling the door shut behind them. The waterfowl had quieted for the night, and the only sound was the rustling of leaves high in the trees. Zach walked to the rear of the cabin where his father had built an addition, a spare room for tools and other items Winona didn't want cluttering up the cabin. Included were the Newhouse traps that Nate once relied on for his livelihood.

"What are you after?" Lou asked, suspecting his intent. She had been in the spare room before.

Hanging from pegs were ten large beaver traps, handmade by the famous firm started by Sewell Newhouse, a New Yorker who early on had seen the potential in the beaver trade for someone able to produce a product trappers could rely on. His became the standard by which all other traps were judged.

Zach helped himself to three of them, along with a trio of stout stakes and a heavy sledge hammer propped by the entrance.

Lou offered to carry the traps, a task she'd routinely performed for her father when he ran his trapline—up to the day hostiles slew him. She knew the trade inside out: how to set a trap, how to bait it, how to skin beaver, everything.

Two trails led into the clearing, the one that linked the cabin to the lake and another from out of the wood to the west. But Zach doubted the prowler used either. He selected a spot where the vegetation grew close to the cabin and proceeded to scoop out a hollow depression with his hands. Into it he placed a trap. Stepping on the springs, he lowered the jaws and delicately adjusted the pan so the slightest pressure would release it.

As Zach was placing blades of grass over the jaws to disguise them, Louisa leaned over his shoulder. "Won't your scent scare it off?"

"Could be," Zach allowed, "but I'm counting on this"—from a pocket he took a sweetcake, which he broke into thirds—"to make the thing so curious, it can't resist." After sprinkling crumbs around the edge of the trap, he put what was left between the jaws, near the pan. "There. What do you think?"

"Clever." Although Louisa was well-versed in the trapping trade, she never had liked it much. She understood the necessity, and had helped her pa because it was expected, but many a night she had lain under her blankets imagining what it must be like for helpless beaver whose legs were snared, struggling futilely as they slowly drowned to death. She'd had to steel herself against becoming too emotional. Once, when they'd caught a young one, she'd touched its head and inwardly prayed for forgiveness, and her father had noticed.

"Why so sad, girl? You don't cry when you eat a slab of beef or ham, do you? This is no different. It's not like we're killing a pet."

"I know, Pa," Lou answered, "but I can't help pitying them."

"For an overgrown rat with a paddle tail?" Her father had walked over and given the dead beaver a kick. "Animals don't think like we do, they don't have souls or go to heaven or any of that. They're just *animals*. Our Maker put them on this earth for us to do with as we see fit. You should never feel guilt over killing one. It's just the way things are."

David Thompson

"I suppose," Lou said, although she'd supposed nothing of the kind. The way things were was wrong. For anything to die was awful. Her mother's death had taught her that.

"Listen, I know this is hard on you." Her father had given her shoulder a squeeze. "It'd be hard on anyone. I'm sorry we don't have a nice home. I'm sorry we couldn't afford to send you to one of those fancy schools for young ladies." He'd gazed wistfully into the distance. "I'm sorry for a lot of things. But I won't be sorry for long. A couple of trapping seasons is all it'll take. We'll have enough money saved for a small place of our own, and maybe enough for school and proper dresses and whatnot."

"School isn't important."

"You're wrong. The right schooling can mean the difference between a life of poverty and the lap of luxury." He'd shaken his wet left leg. "Why do you think I'm doing this? Why do I spend hours in icy water every day, half froze? Why do I break my back toting heavy beaver? Why am I in these godforsaken mountains, where hostiles wouldn't think twice about separating me from my hair? For you, girl. It's all for you. So you'll have the kind of life I never did."

Lou wished he hadn't told her that. All those dead beaver—they died on her account! She'd felt worse than ever.

Now, as Zach King roved the edge of the trees in search of another spot to set a trap, Lou hoped that whatever was caught wouldn't suffer very much.

Setting the last two traps took longer than Zach had anticipated. By the time he was done, the forest was blanketed in blackness. Myriad stars filled the firmament, bright grains of sand in a limitless ethereal sea.

Lou was reveling in the spectacle. "I can never get over how close they seem up here. It's almost as if we can reach out and touch them."

"When I was little I tried to hit the moon with an arrow," Zach disclosed.

"You did?" Lou tittered gaily.

"Pa gave me a small bow when I was six or seven. One night

54

I saw a full moon through the window and came outside. It looked so close, I shot at it.'' Zach didn't know why he was telling her. He'd never shared the embarrassing story with anyone.

"I can just see you," Lou teased, "in your little loincloth, aiming your little bow. How cute!''

"Pa didn't think so. There was a grizzly grunting and coughing off in the brush. I didn't pay it much mind. But it woke up Pa, and he saw I was missing and came out to fetch me. Otherwise, I might not be standing here right now.''

Lou had been holding his rifle so he could wield the sledge. Suddenly she felt an overpowering sensation, a feeling that they were being watched, and she swung around, leveling the Hawken. She thought she saw a pair of fiery eyes deep in the undergrowth. But they blinked out before she could determine what they really were. "I think I saw something.''

"What?" Zach scanned the gloom.

"I'm not sure.''

"Let's go see, then.'' With the big hammer poised to swing, Zach started toward the pines.

"No!" Lou cried much louder than she intended. Fear gnawed at her innards, fear she couldn't fathom. Raw fright so potent she almost seized him to stop him from going another inch.

Zach halted, puzzled. She'd been acting peculiar all evening, and he didn't know what to make of it. "Why are you so blamed skittish?''

"I wish I knew.'' Lou sincerely did. The fear issued from deep down within her, from her very core, and was unlike any she'd ever experienced.

Of two minds, Zach hesitated. He had no qualms about going into the forest. Truth was, being alone with her awhile would fulfill a craving he'd had all day. But her expression gave him pause. She was intensely troubled. It might be best to take her back inside. His desire waged war with his conscience, and his conscience won. "As jumpy as you are, you're liable to shoot me by mistake. So let's go on in.''

Lou wasn't fooled. He was joking to put her at ease, but he

was really concerned, and he was going back inside for her sake. It was so sweet. Love flooded through her, washing out the fear. She was tempted to throw her arms around his neck and smother him with hot kisses, but she settled for taking his hand. "Thank you."

"For what?"

"For being you."

Touch the Clouds was being shadowed. Someone, or something, was after him. He'd become aware of it late in the afternoon, and the conviction had grown as the day gave way to night. No sounds had given the shadower away. Rather, the lack of sounds had. The lack of chirping birds, of chattering squirrels and chipmunks. He'd not seen a single living creature since he left the burning lodge of Talks to Himself.

The huge Shoshone suspected the cause and was gripped by an emotion new to him: dread. Bears and panthers and enemy warriors he could contend with. But the thing stalking him now was neither man nor beast but a savage mix, a creature out of legend, a creature so evil, Shoshone mothers only had to mention it to scare their offsprings into complying with their wishes. "Never wander off alone or the NunumBi will get you!" was a warning his own mother had resorted to when he was a boy.

The NunumBi. Even now, even with all Touch the Clouds had witnessed at Talks to Himself's, he couldn't believe it.

His camp lay in a grassy, windswept meadow, out in the open, where nothing could approach without him knowing it. His fire was the twice the size it should be, another precaution. Beside him, on either side, were his lance and bow.

From encircling slopes wafted the wavering wail of wolves, the throaty yips of coyotes, the screams of big cats, and the grunts of marauding bears. Night was when the predators ruled, when smaller animals quaked in their burrows. Until dawn the shrieks of prey would punctuate the feral chorus.

Touch the Clouds and those smaller creatures had something in common. He was being stalked just as they were. All his life he had been the hunter, not the hunted, and he didn't like having the roles reversed.

The high grass rustled, as it had been doing since the breeze picked up. Touch the Clouds saw blade tops ripple in a straight line from south to north. But the wind was blowing from the northwest.

Two of the horses whinnied; another pulled at the tether. Rising, Touch the Clouds calmed them, stroking each and speaking softly. His presence reassured them, but as soon as he returned to the fire they acted up again.

To be stranded afoot would be a calamity. The elk meat, piled high across the fire, would be left to rot, and the potential loss angered him. Not so much because of all the trouble he had gone to obtaining it, but because his family would be deprived of food they might greatly need during the upcoming winter.

"I defy you, NunumBi," Touch the Clouds said aloud.

As if in reply, the grass rustled anew, stems bending nearer to the camp. They stopped rustling short of where the ring of light penetrated. Bending, Touch the Clouds gripped the end of a burning brand, then dashed into the grass, waving it in front of him. He came to where he was positive the NunumBi would be, but found nothing.

Had it merely been the wind? the Shoshone questioned his judgment. Was his fear as groundless as a child's who was afraid of the dark? Were all his instincts wrong? Had his warrior's training failed him?

No! Touch the Clouds spied a pair of burning coals. Not in the fire, but to the north a stone's throw from where he stood. "Come for me, if you dare!" he challenged. "I am ready!"

Only, he wasn't. He had foolishly left the lance and bow by the fire. All he had with him was his long knife. With a start, he darted toward his weapons. The eyes were gone, but the grass was rippling again, bending toward him as the creatures rushed to intercept him. Rotating, he swung the burning brand and back-pedaled, unwilling to turn his back to the thing.

The moment Touch the Clouds stepped into the circle of light, the grass stopped moving. The old stories were true, then. Touch the Clouds smiled grimly. It wasn't hopeless. He had a chance if he didn't let down his guard. Whooping in glee, he hopped from leg to leg, as much to bolster his own confidence as to show the monstrosity in the grass he had not been cowed.

A raspy growl was the reaction, low and ripe with menace; the coals briefly shone scarlet.

Dipping onto one knee, Touch the Clouds swiftly notched a feathered shaft to the sinew string. His movements were a blur. The string against his cheek, he sighted down the arrow, aiming between the close-spaced orbs. His fingers relaxed and the string hummed. Faster than the human eye could follow, the shaft streaked at the apparition. The barbed tip cleaved the grass like a sword tip, but no outcry was forthcoming, no roar of rage or anguish resounded.

Touch the Clouds knew he'd missed, though not through any fault of his. The arrow had flown true, but the NunumBi was no longer there. It had vanished as if swallowed by the earth, just as the legends claimed it could. Perplexed, he lowered the bow—and there the eyes were again, not three paces to the right of where they had been. Annoyed, he whipped another arrow from his quiver and let fly with blinding speed, speed few Shoshones could rival, speed that had kept the Piegans and the Sioux at bay. Yet it wasn't quick enough. Once more the creature melted into empty air and was gone.

In combat Touch the Clouds had always prevailed. His sinews had been equal to every onslaught. On those few occasions when brute brawn had not been enough to triumph, his wits had seen him through. But now neither were effective. The abomination in the dark was more than his match; it was his better.

The thought galvanized Touch the Clouds into springing to the elk meat and lifting one of the heavy packs. He had made a grave mistake in stopping for the night. By doing so he had set himself up as a roosting sage hen, waiting to be plucked. But it wasn't too late. He could throw on the packs and leave.

As he turned toward the five horses, the one at the other end of the string snorted and reared. Then the second did the same. And the third.

Dropping the bundle, Touch the Clouds bounded to their aid. Low to the ground a hairy form flashed. The remaining horses plunged and squealed. A sibilant snarl lent impetus to their panic and they wrenched at the rope in a frenzy. Touch the Clouds was almost to them, his arm outstretched, when the stake shot from the ground as if shot from a rifle, narrowly missing his temple as it whizzed by.

The metal stake had been a gift from Grizzly Killer. "So the Sioux won't steal your warhorse out from under your nose," he'd bantered. "Picket pins" was how the whites referred to them.

Touch the Clouds always cherished his as a token of the depth of their friendship. Now he lunged, his left hand grasping the end. Coated with loose dirt, it was as slippery as ice. He couldn't hold on. The next second the horses, the rope, and the stake were rapidly retreating across the meadow and he was on his stomach, the bow pinned under his chest, helpless to prevent their flight.

Heaving onto his knees, Touch the Clouds swiveled. In the grass gleamed the bloodred coals, locked on him in undisguised spite. Hatred so powerful it buffeted him like waves of heat. Or was it another illusion spawned by his rising fear? For yes, Touch the Clouds was scared, scared as he had never been before. All the old tales filled his head, the horrible stories, the gory accounts, the dire warnings.

The coals flew toward him.

Touch the Clouds scrambled erect, snagging the lance as he rose. He cocked his arm but didn't throw. The thing must come closer. It must be so close he could see the vertical slits in its eyes. So close he couldn't miss.

But just like the last time, the creature stopped shy of the firelight. A feline screech rent the night. Frustration or anger, Touch the Clouds couldn't say. Twice the firelight had saved him, but would it a third time? He decided not to remain and find out. Slinging the bow over his shoulder, he held the lance in one hand and a new burning brand in the other.

David Thompson

The NunumBi hadn't moved. Touch the Clouds glanced eastward, at a stand of trees. Then he flung the brand at the creature, spun on the ball of his left foot, and fled, bounding like a blacktail buck.

The warrior half hoped the grass would catch on fire. It might drive the creature off, might enable him to escape. A glance showed the brand sputtering, the flames almost extinguished by the force of his throw. The eyes were gone, so maybe he had succeeded anyway.

Any such hope was dashed by a slash of red to the south of the camp. Touch the Clouds realized the creature was in pursuit, that it was skirting the fire. He gauged the distance to the trees and then the distance between his pursuer and himself, and calculated he wouldn't make it. The thing would be on him before he got there.

Among the Shoshones footraces were popular. Touch the Clouds was by no means the fleetest runner in the tribe, but he was one of the swiftest and had distinguished himself in competition both with his own people and the whites. Tonight he ran as if his heels were endowed with wings, as if he were living lightning. It wasn't enough.

The NunumBi narrowed the gap at an astounding rate. Only an antelope could outrun it, if that. Grass parted before the creature like water before the prow of a canoe, its blazing eyes hurtling closer, ever closer.

Touch the Clouds hurled the lance as soon as the thing came within striking range. In a fluid, practiced tactic, he whirled and threw, marshaling all the strength in his sinews. Enough to impale a buffalo. Not waiting to see the effect, he resumed running toward the trees, so near yet so far. He didn't look back again. To do so might make him break stride or stumble, and either would prove fatal.

Legs pounding, the Shoshone grinned as the trees reared up out of the murk, some with stout limbs low enough for him to grab. His elation proved short-lived, however, for on his ears fell the sound of heaving breathing, like the labored wheezing of a grizzly.

Another few strides and Touch the Clouds launched himself at the trees. His fingers were hooked for purchase, his spine arched. He concentrated on one of the branches to the exclusion of all else—until razor claws sheared into his lower leg.

Chapter Five

Zach King's eyes snapped open and he bolted upright. A faint sound had intruded on his sleep. He stayed where he was, attuning his senses to his surroundings as his father had taught him. On the bed across the room his parents slumbered, his mother snoring lightly. In the opposite corner slept his sister and Lou, both so bundled in blankets he couldn't see either. Through the window filtered a pale glow, heralding the dawn to come. It was almost morning.

Zach immediately thought of his traps and wondered if he had caught the skulker. The sound that had awakened him wasn't repeated, so he couldn't venture a guess as to what it had been. Tossing off the top blankets, he donned his buckskins and moccasins and armed himself.

On cat's feet Zach tiptoed from the cabin, easing the door shut so the hinges wouldn't creak. A brisk chill pervaded the valley and gooseflesh crawled over him as he hustled past the corner toward one of the beaver traps. Right away he saw that it had been sprung. But nothing was in it. The jaws were empty. And the piece of sweetcake he'd left next to the pan was gone.

David Thompson

Zach ran to the next trap. The situation was the same, only in this instance a thick stick was caught tight. The trap had been deliberately triggered. And once again the sweetcake was missing.

"I'll be damned," Zach said under his breath, the full implication hitting him like a war club. It couldn't be an animal. Despite the teeth marks on the bridles, it had to be a person. He jogged to the last beaver trap and wasn't surprised to find it had also been sprung and the bait removed.

Zach scoured the vegetation, baffled. Whoever it was, they were toying with him. Taunting him. They must have watched him set the traps. Lou's jumpiness the previous night had been justified. Remembering the tack shed, he hurried there. The door was still shut and betrayed no sign of tampering. So the log was still in place.

Some of the horses were dozing, others eating from the trough. Zach's mount, a sorrel, clomped over to nuzzle him and be stroked. "How am I going to catch this devil?" he puzzled aloud.

Depressed, Zach headed for the lake. His morning ritual called for a dip in the freezing-cold water. Afterward, a hearty breakfast courtesy of his mother, then the day's work would commence.

A golden crown invested the eastern sky with color. Birds were breaking out in cheery song, and as Zach came down the trail he spotted several deer and two elk, drinking. Automatically he brought up his Hawken, then just as promptly lowered it. His father had standing instructions to the effect that they were to kill only game in close proximity to the lake when they couldn't find it anywhere else. Zach rated it a silly waste until his father elaborated: "If we start shooting all the game that comes to drink, pretty soon we'll have killed off all the deer and elk in our valley. Then we'll have to go farther afield. Now, I don't know about you, but in the middle of winter, the last thing I want is to ride thirty miles through deep snow just to find fresh meat."

The two elk and the deer didn't catch wind of Zach until he was almost to the shore. Snorting, they crashed off through the brush, as did a pair of mountain sheep he hadn't noticed. Striding to the lake's edge, he set his guns to one side, stripped out of his clothes, and plunged in.

The icy water jolted Zach, jangling his nervous system. Any lingering vestige of sleepiness was obliterated. He swam twenty feet out, bent, and dived, stroking cleanly. Fish scurried away, glimmers of silver and brown. Bracing his feet on the bottom, he uncoiled and shot to the surface.

Many of the stars were gone, relinquishing their celestial posts to the advent of day. The sun had yet to rise, but its rays bathed half the sky.

Zach floated on his back and idly kicked toward shore. He had much to think about, foremost how he would snare the intruder. Zach raised his head. That was it! *A snare!* Better yet, a double snare! He chuckled at his cleverness, rotated, and swam the rest of the way.

Rising out of the lake, Zach walked to where he had left his clothes and started to lower himself to the ground. He saw his rifle and his pistols and his ammo pouch and powder horn—but not his buckskins. For several seconds he gaped, unwilling to credit his own eyes. His clothes were gone! Someone had taken them!

Zach's first thought was that his sister was playing a prank. It would be just like Evelyn to swipe his buckskins and make him traipse naked to the cabin. Only thing was, she rarely got up before sunrise. She was the sleepyhead of the family, never stirring outdoors until it had warmed up. That left Lou, who'd often joked how she couldn't wait to see him without his clothes. Smirking, Zach checked the trail, then faced the woods. "All right, you scamp. Bring them back."

She offered no response.

"Did you hear me?" Zach raised his voice. "What if one of my parents see me like this? They might think we're misbehaving."

Still no reply.

Zach made no attempt to cover himself. If she wanted a good look, let her have one. He wasn't like those missionaries he'd met at the rendezvous, the ones who claimed bare flesh was sinful. How could that be when everyone was *born* naked? "Louisa, where are you? Enough is enough."

A clump of tall weeds shook. Laughing, Zach dashed toward it, thinking to teach her a lesson; he'd tackle her and tickle her until she begged for mercy. Suddenly his buckskin shirt sailed out of the weeds, landing in front of him. He checked his rush. The shirt had been slashed and torn from top to bottom.

Zach's pulse quickened. It wasn't his fiancée. It was the scoundrel who had destroyed their tack! Who had made a jackass of him by setting off the traps! Spinning, he ran to his pistols and scooped them up. "You're not getting away this time!"

The weeds were still shaking. Zach raced toward them, heedless of the stones that gouged the soles of his feet. He was four yards away when they stopped moving. Four measly yards. Yet when he barreled into them and looked right and left, only his pants were there, untouched.

"Where in the world—?" Zach blurted. There hadn't been time for the culprit to escape, but no one was in sight. Sprinting farther, he searched behind trees and boulders, logs and thickets. The ground yielded no tracks. Confusion beset Zach. None of it made sense. Why steal his clothes but leave his guns? Why taunt him by literally flinging the shirt in his face? And how had the thief disappeared from right under his nose?

The sun was rising. Admitting defeat, Zach pulled on his pants. Whoever he was up against was no ordinary woodsman. They possessed skill unlike any he'd encountered, and that included the wily Apaches his family tangled with on a visit to Santa Fe. In a sense, Lou had been right. They were dealing with a ghost.

What galled Zach most was how he was being made to look the fool. The traps, his shirt, they were all intentional affronts. Maybe the bridles and saddles had been, too. Maybe—the notion staggered him—maybe the whole series of events, from the taking of the ax to this latest incident, were done to make his whole family out to be idiots. It smacked of pure and utter wickedness.

Then and there, Zach resolved he'd had enough. Two could

play at that game, as his father's people were fond of saying. He was clever, too, and he would prove it by catching the skulker. The big question was how to go about it.

A shout up at the cabin motivated Zach to pull on his moccasins, drape his powder horn and ammo pouch across his chest, and scurry up the trail. Halfway there, he met his beloved coming down.

Louisa had risen to the fragrant aroma of coffee being brewed. Winona was at the fireplace, Nate at the table. When she saw Zach was gone, she slipped into her clothes under her blanket, then ran a quill brush through her hair and scooted outside, saying, "We'll be back in time for breakfast."

A circuit of the clearing revealed Zach was elsewhere. The lake, she reasoned, and she was elated to see him unharmed but puzzled as to why he had on only his britches. When he held up his torn shirt, her puzzlement grew. "How did that happen?"

"How do you think?" he rejoined, and detailed its fate. "The thing is probably watching us this very second. Just like it was last night when I set the traps."

Somehow, Lou doubted it. She wasn't experiencing the horrid sensation she had before.

"I don't want my folks to know," Zach said. "Ma will raise a fuss. Say it's too dangerous for me to try and catch this thing." Walking slowly, they hiked homeward.

She might be right, Lou reflected. To him she said, "Maybe it's best if we leave it for your father and Shakespeare McNair. Between the two of them, they've caught every critter under the sun. They know how to go about it."

"And I don't?" Zach said, miffed by the slight.

"I didn't say that. Why are you always putting words into my mouth?" It was one of his less desirable traits. "All I'm saying is that it could be too much for you to handle by your lonesome."

Zach didn't know which was worse, being branded dumb or no-account. "I'm not alone. I have you to help me. That is, if

67

you're still with me. If not, let me know now. I won't hold it against you."

Lou had a hunch he would do that very thing. He wasn't the kind to hold grudges, but neither did he forget slights. "I'll always stand by your side. Come what may," she stressed.

Zach stopped and faced her. Swinging the tattered shirt over a shoulder, he looped his arm around her slender waist and pulled her close. As always, the contact of her body with his was like being struck by a bolt of lightning. He flushed scalding hot, his mouth went dry, and the world was blotted out of existence by a dazzling haze. His mouth lowered to hers, their lips molding as if they were two halves of the same coin.

Lou flung her arms around his neck and shamelessly pressed tight against him. She had no reservations about it. They were to be wed, to be joined eternally as husband and wife. As far as she was concerned, she was his now and forevermore. Not that she would let him have complete sway, however. As her mother had endlessly impressed on her, there were some things a young lady didn't do. Not ever. One of those was to surrender her body totally. That was for the night after their vows—for when a girl could give of herself secure in the knowledge that the precious gift she was sharing was highly valued.

Zach was marveling at how he could never get enough of her. She tasted like honey, her scent like a field of flowers. Louisa was the sum and substance of his innermost desires, all that he had ever imagined he would want in a girl and so much more. Kissing her was bliss. He never wanted to stop.

Lou ran her fingertips across his neck and felt him quiver. She liked how responsive he was. She enjoyed exciting him. He had the same effect on her. Adrift in rapture, she couldn't wait until the day they were finally man and wife to consummate their union.

"If only Pa and Ma could see you now."

Zach jerked back as if he had been stabbed. The smug smirk on his sister's face irritated him no end. "How long have you been watching us?"

"Not long," Evelyn said. Bundled in a small robe, she would have rather been under her blankets, toasty and content. But her mother had sent her to deliver a message. "It's time to come up and eat."

"Thank you," Louisa said, her cheeks burning.

Evelyn wondered why her brother wasn't wearing his shirt, but she didn't pry. He and Lou did a lot of peculiar things, a lot of it having to do with matters she didn't care to know about. Frankly, her brother had been easier to live with and easier to understand when all he was interested in was hunting and becoming a famous warrior. "Food's getting cold," she said, marching off.

Zach reached for Lou again. "I'm not hungry."

"No. We'd better go." Lou swatted his hands aside. "They'll brand me a hussy, us kissing in broad daylight."

Reluctantly, Zach dogged her heels. He could use another dip in the lake to cool off. The morning had gotten off to a bad start, which some of his Shoshone friends would take as an omen. But he wasn't superstitious. The rest of the day would go better because he would *make* it go better.

Then they came to the cabin and Nate was waiting, rubbing the back of his head, a pained expression on his face. "There you are."

"Something wrong, Pa?" Zach inquired.

"My head is throbbing like the dickens."

"Why?" Zach asked, even though he had a fair idea.

"Someone propped a log over the door inside the tack shed and didn't tell the rest of us. You wouldn't happen to have any idea who?"

Evelyn was none too happy. She'd had to wash the breakfast dishes *and* the supper dishes from last night. Which wasn't fair. Zach and she always took turns, but Zach had forgotten to do the supper dishes because he was out setting his stupid traps. Or that was the excuse he gave their parents.

There were days when Evelyn couldn't comprehend why the

David Thompson

Almighty had seen fit to inflict a brother on her. Why not a sister? A girl like Louisa would be a lot of fun. Someone who wouldn't boss her around or treat her like she was a nuisance.

In the lazy heat of midafternoon, Evelyn strolled around the clearing, bored to death. She liked to play in the woods, but her folks wouldn't let her. It wasn't safe, they said. Not with all that had been going on.

Zach's shirt had been the last straw. Her mother had been fit to spit rocks, and her father had taken Zach and gone off to hunt the prowler down. "We're not waiting for McNair," he had announced. "We're ending it now before someone is hurt."

Evelyn wasn't as upset as everyone else. To her mind, if whoever was doing all the bad stuff wanted to hurt them, the person could have done it at any time. No, she was more disturbed by the little man in the cave.

For the life of her, Evelyn couldn't see how she had been mistaken. It had been the middle of the afternoon, just like now, and she had seen the little man as clearly as she saw the cabin. The hole in the ground, the wrinkled figure, they had been real. For her father to doubt her, for her parents to think she had made the whole thing up in her head, was almost enough to make her cry.

Somehow, Evelyn had to show them she had been telling the truth. But how, when the cave and the small man were gone? Depressed, she moved toward a log in the shade, a log she had roosted on many times. Not paying much attention, she didn't notice the object lying on it until she was about to sit down.

"What's this doing here?"

A small piece of sweetcake rested in the very center. Suspecting her brother was up to no good, Evelyn looked around. She was alone. Along with blackberry pie, Evelyn relished her mother's delicious sweetcakes most, so without delay she picked it up and stuffed it into her mouth. The piece was dry and crumbled apart, but it was as tasty as any other. Smacking her lips, Evelyn began to sit when her gaze alighted on another piece of sweetcake about ten hops and a jump into the trees.

"What's going on?"

More convinced than ever that her brother was behind it, Evelyn cautiously entered the forest. She was disobeying her parents, but it was only to treat herself to the morsel. It occurred to her that maybe Zach had left it as a test, to see whether she was brave enough to go in the woods on her own. It also occurred to her that she shouldn't, that if her folks caught her she would be punished. But it was only a short way—and she did so crave sweetcake.

A heavy stillness hung over the valley, not at all unusual at that time of day. Bands of sunlight and shadow dappled the earth, and a dank scent filled Evelyn's nostrils. She had to brush some specks of dirt off the second piece before she could take a bite. Like the first, it was quite dry.

A glass of water was in order. Licking her fingers, Evelyn was on the verge of shifting when she spotted yet another piece of cake even farther into the undergrowth. It lay in a clear patch close to a dense thicket. Her ridiculously stupid brother had gone to a lot of effort, but it was all right by her. When it came to sweetcake she was a bottomless pit. Skipping toward it, she thought of the times she had used the same trick to lure birds. She'd make a trail of bread crumbs leading right up to her hiding place, and the birds would come so close she could reach out and touch them. Or try to. Most were amazingly quick and usually flew off before she could grab them. Once she caught hold of a sparrow and tried to pet it, but it wouldn't stop thrashing and chirping, so she'd let it go.

Hunkering, Evelyn bit into the third piece and said, "Mmmmmm!" real loud, just in case her brother was spying on her. She wanted him to know how much she liked his latest game. "Thanks!" she called out, and giggled.

That was when a strange feeling came over her. A feeling that she was indeed being watched. A feeling so strong, she didn't doubt it was true. Glancing up, she searched but saw no one. As her eyes roved over the thicket, though, a shape deep within the shadows caught her interest. It might be a small log, but it was taller than it was wide and the upper part resembled a small head and neck.

Evelyn wondered if it was an animal, a coon or a possum or maybe a marmot. Leaning forward, she sought to get a better view but the shadows hindered her. "Howdy, little critter," she said good-naturedly. She had always liked animals.

The thing moved. Evelyn distinctly saw it change position and rise higher. Eyelids blinked. Eyes that glowed a dim, pale shade of red appeared. That worried her until she recollected that at night the eyes of animals often glowed when light from a lantern or a fire shone on them.

"What are you, little fella? Come out where I can see you."

The animal moved toward her, but only a few shuffling steps. Evelyn held out the last of the sweetcake. "Here? Want a bite? I'll let you eat right out of my hand." She had fed chipmunks and squirrels that way, and a friendly possum that used to come around periodically.

The thing stayed where it was.

"Pretty please," Evelyn coaxed, beckoning. To her astonishment, the creature raised a limb and imitated her, beckoning to her as she'd just done. "I'll be!" she exclaimed. She'd never seen the like.

Back when Evelyn's mother was young, another Shoshone girl had tamed a raccoon and taught it all kinds of tricks. It would sit on the girl's lap, roll over on command, rub its paws together, and even cover its eyes like it was playing hide-and-seek. Evelyn always wished she had a coon of her own, or any animal that would do the same.

"Come on. Don't be afraid. I'm harmless."

The animal made a sound. Sort of a cross between the whine of a puppy and the mew of a kitten.

Evelyn laughed. "Does that mean you'd like this treat?" She wagged the sweetcake and smacked her lips. "It's better than any old bugs or frogs or whatever you usually eat." Bending until she nearly tipped over, she eased her arm into the thicket so as not to alarm it.

The thing moved a bit nearer.

"You'll have to come closer than that," Evelyn said. "I can't reach any farther." She couldn't make out what it was beyond noting that it had a lot of hair. She also had the impression it was hunched over, probably because it was afraid. So she sat real quiet.

Again the animal advanced, threading through the thicket with ease.

The growth was so thick, the limbs so interwoven, that Evelyn couldn't see how the creature moved so freely. A mouse would have trouble making its way through that maze. Clasping the piece of cake so it was at the ends of her fingers, she patiently waited for her prospective new pet to take it.

A new sound fell on her ears, a low trilling, or purring, like a sound a cat would make. The eyes had stopped glowing, or had they? Evelyn could see two thin reddish slits. It must have had its eyes almost shut, but that was ridiculous.

Only a couple of feet separated them, yet Evelyn still couldn't determine what kind of animal it was. The shape was all wrong for a raccoon. And the body was too thin to be a possum or a marmot.

The thing had halted and was swaying from side to side, a sign it was too scared to come the rest of the way.

"Just a little more," Evelyn cooed. "Take this piece and I'll fetch you more. We can be great friends, the two of us. Like my brother and his wolf were."

Years before, Zach had befriended a wolf cub and raised it as his own, and the two had shared a special bond. Wherever Zach went, the wolf went. Whatever Zach did, the wolf was always right at his side. Evelyn had envied him no end. Then one day the wolf heard some of its kind howling up in the mountains, and not long after, it ran off. From time to time it would visit Zach, but each stay was shorter than the last until finally it loped off, never to return. Her father said it was just being true to its nature, that wolves weren't meant to be cooped up in cabins or fed out of pans. They had to run wild and free.

David Thompson

A rustling noise ended Evelyn's reverie. She was shocked to discover the creature was now an arm's length away. As luck would have it, the spot where it stood was in the shadow of a nearby tree. She tingled with anticipation as its shoulders moved and a paw rose toward the sweetcake. Another couple of inches and she'd have done it!

Suddenly the animal growled.

"Blue Flower! What are you doing?"

Startled, Evelyn glanced over her shoulder. At the edge of the trees was her mother, and her ma didn't look happy. Evelyn turned back to the animal, but it was gone. Into a burrow, she assumed. Yanking her arm from the thicket, she rose, keeping her hands behind her back.

Winona placed her hands on her hips and tapped her foot, irked by her daughter's behavior. Among her people it was unthinkable for a child to disobey a parent. From the cradleboard on, children were taught to always respect the wishes of their elders. "What do you have to say for yourself, young lady?"

"I'm staying close to the cabin like you told me," Evelyn said innocently.

"You weren't to leave the clearing," Winona sternly reminded her. "I made that plain to you. But you did so anyway."

"I only went a little ways."

Winona was in no mood to quibble. "When we say you cannot leave the clearing, we mean just that. You were not to take one step into the forest."

"Ah, Ma." Evelyn wished her mother hadn't spoiled everything. "I can take care of myself."

"No, you cannot," Winona bluntly responded. "Until we find whatever has been coming around, you are not to go anywhere alone. And for disobeying me, you will do all the dishes for the next seven days."

Evelyn clutched her chest. "A whole week? That's not fair."

Winona held up a finger. "One more word and it will be for an entire moon." Her daughter didn't seem to recognize the seriousness of the situation, so for Blue Flower's own sake, she had to be firm. "Now come inside and help me sew."

Miserable as could be, Evelyn glumly obeyed. As they turned the corner she gave the thicket a last look and could have sworn she glimpsed a pair of shiny red eyes.

Chapter Six

Evening descended on the Rocky Mountains. The shadows of jagged peaks cast lower slopes in murky twilight. Lakes, ponds, and rivers that were bright blue during the day acquired duskier hues. The deep woods were plunged in gloom. All along the front range animals were on the move, the grass-eaters seeking shelter for the night, the meat-eaters leaving their dens to stretch and go in quest of prey.

But in the Kings' valley not so much as a caterpillar stirred. All day Nate had noted an absence of wildlife, and it alarmed him that their absence was most obvious in the immediate vicinity of the cabin. All the birds, all the squirrels, all the chipmunks were gone. He hadn't seen a rabbit or deer since morning.

Something was wrong, dreadfully wrong. A lack of game meant a large predator was abroad, but he had long since eliminated all grizzlies and mountain lions, and Winona had killed the last wolverine.

His horses added to the ominous portents. Since late afternoon they had stood huddled in a corner of the corral closest to the cabin, their rumps against the rails, their ears pricked toward the woods.

Something was out there, something that frightened them. A threat that caused even Nate's big stallion to act like a timid foal. Their nervousness had grown with each passing hour, and by evening they were constantly nickering, their eyes wide, their nostrils flared.

Nate shared their apprehension. Danger loomed, danger to his family, to those who were his whole life. It was frustrating beyond measure, not knowing what form the danger would take or when it would strike.

Seated on a stump at the clearing's border, Hawken across his thighs, Nate stared out over his private domain. This valley was his home. Eighteen years earlier he'd claimed it for his own and held on to it, defying repeated attempts by the Utes and others to drive him out. In all that time, none of the threats he faced were as unnerving as this new one.

Confronting a known enemy was one thing, confronting an elusive foe who defied his every attempt to track it down, another. Nate had no notion of who or what he was up against, and it was that, more than the absence of wildlife and the terrified horses, that disturbed him most. How could he protect his loved ones when he had no clue what he was protecting them from? How could he defend his domain when it had been invaded by a will-o'-the-wisp?

A destructive will-o'-the-wisp. An adversary who grew increasingly brazen, as the shredding of his son's shirt demonstrated. How long, Nate fretted, before the skulker in the forest vented its violent urges on people instead of objects? How long before someone he cared for was harmed?

Soft footsteps jarred Nate's thoughts. He arced the Hawken's muzzle toward the source and found himself pointing the rifle at his wife. "Sorry," he said, hastily letting the barrel droop. "I didn't realize it was you."

Winona had seen him from a window. He had been facing the other way, but she could tell by his posture he was tense and troubled. "It is not like you, husband, to jump at shadows."

"I am a mite edgy," Nate admitted. He didn't say why. There was no need.

Taking hold of his hand, Winona pressed it to her lips. "Calm yourself. No one has been hurt."

"Yet."

Of males' many traits that confounded Winona, their knack for focusing on the worst that could happen was one of the foremost. Women were much more apt to look at the rosy side of things. "I have complete confidence in you. Just remember. We are a family. We oppose our enemies together."

Nate motioned for her to sit, then squatted beside the stump. "I've been thinking. Maybe you should take Zach and the girls and go visit your people." The sharp look she bestowed on him compelled him to add, "Only for a little while. Until it's safe."

"We are not leaving you," Winona said flatly.

"But—"

She touched a finger to his mouth. "A King does not run out on a King. Are those not your own words? Shoshones, too, put family above all else. How would my relatives treat me if they learned I had deserted you when you were in need?" She shook her head, her luxurious raven hair swirling. "No. I stay. Warriors are not the only ones who must show courage in a crisis."

Nate was prepared for her argument. "If not for your own sake, do it for Zach, Evelyn, and Lou."

"Our children have always stood by us when we are in peril. Remember when Blue Flower was a baby and Stalking Coyote saved her from those killers? And how our son held his own in Blackfoot country?" Winona beamed proudly. "They are like their father in that they do not run from difficulty. They face it. They conquer it."

Nate had saved the most important point for last. His voice broke as he said it, for to confess that he was less than he should be tore at the fabric of his manhood. "I don't know if I can protect them."

"You will do your best, as you always do. More than that we cannot ask."

"Didn't you hear me, Winona? I can't promise you they'll live through this. Whatever we're up against is more than a match for me. So far it's only toyed with us. But what if it chooses to rip up one of our kids instead of some saddles?" Nate paused. *"I can't stop it."*

"Nonsense. It is flesh and blood, like we are. So it can be killed, just as we can. Perhaps alone you cannot stop it, but you are not alone. You have all of us to help you. Together, we will beat it."

"How can I talk sense into you when you've already made up your mind?" Nate complained. Experience had taught him that once she did, he'd have to move heaven and earth to get her to change it. And he didn't have the time to spare. They had to get the younger ones out of there before it was too late.

"It is settled, then."

Nate refused to concede. "It's nothing of the sort. I'll have a talk with each of them." He could convince Zach to spirit Louisa away to spare her. As for Evelyn, she had a stubborn streak like her mother, but she never could refuse him when he asked nicely.

Winona bent so they were nose to nose, then pecked him on the cheek. Running her fingers through his beard, she gripped his chin. "Husband, in all the winters we have been together I have never doubted you. I have never questioned your judgment. But I say to you, this time you are wrong."

"I don't want them hurt," Nate emphasized.

"And I do?" Winona put her forehead against his. "Shakespeare McNair and you like to joke that women think with their hearts and not their heads. I ask you, which one of us is doing that now?" She didn't give him the opportunity to answer. "You are worried because you love us. We love you, too, and are just as worried about you. Together, united, our love will be the glue that binds us in our hardship. Together we will prevail, or together we will fall. The important thing is that we stand by one another, that we live or die as a *family*."

The depth of her devotion brought a lump to Nate's throat, and he coughed. "You're the greatest gift the good Lord ever gave me. You, and Zach and Evelyn. I'd feel better if all of you were well away from here."

"And what of us? I would not sleep until you were in my arms again. Stalking Coyote would never forgive you for treating him as if he were not worthy to fight by your side. And Blue Flower would shed countless tears." Winona stroked his brow. "We have a right to be with you. If you care for us as much as you say, you will not deny us."

"Damn it," Nate said, closing his eyes. Everything she said was true, but she was asking him to willingly agree to their possible slaughter. What man in his right mind would do that?

"Please, husband. For us."

Turmoil churned in Nate like a leaf in a tornado. He had to say no. He just had to.

"For us," a voice echoed.

"Yes, Pa," for us," chimed in another.

"Count me in, too."

Nate straightened and rotated. They were all present, Zach and Lou holding hands, Evelyn appealing to him with those adorable doe eyes of hers. The ones who meant more to him than anything or anyone. His family.

The word pealed in Nate's head like bells in a steeple. *Family.* It was the single most important achievement in a person's life, to have a family of their own. It was the measure of their maturity. Were he to deny his, were he to send the four of them packing, it would be the same as saying his family wasn't strong enough to weather the current adversity. It would be the same as declaring his family a failure. The insight staggered him inwardly.

"Are you all right, Pa?" Evelyn asked.

"We won't go, Pa," Zach said. "Even if you make us, we'll turn around and come right back. Our place is at your side, just like Ma says."

Lou had a comment, too. "I might be speaking out of turn. I'm not officially part of your family yet, but I will be before another year is out. So I have to say I agree with Mrs. King, too. My own pa used to say that kin should always be able to depend on kin, no matter what.''

"Very well, then," Nate said softly, but Zach had started talking and no one heard him.

"If we were up against Blackfeet or Utes you wouldn't send us off. This is no different. It's our valley, isn't it? We've never let hostiles run us off, and we're not about to let this new threat do it, either."

Evelyn thrust her jaw out defiantly. "Yell at us if you want, Pa. But we're not going anywhere unless you do."

Nate had never been prouder of his children than he was at that moment. He'd always believed that a family was the foundation of all a person was and all they became. That the values a person carried through life were the result of the kind of a family they were reared in. Strong families bred strong people. Now his children were confirming that the love and devotion he had lavished on them had reaped the results he'd hoped for. "We'll all stay," he announced.

"How's that?" Zach couldn't remember the last time his father had let them talk him into anything.

"We'll see this through together," Nate clarified. "But there are conditions each of you must abide by."

Evelyn was so elated, she giggled. "Oh, we always listen to you and Ma, Pa. You know that." She saw her mother arch an eyebrow in her direction and hastily added, "Well, most of the time we do."

"No one goes anywhere alone," Nate said. "Always move about in pairs, and always carry a gun. Break the rule and you won't be allowed out of the cabin until the lake freezes over."

"But that's never happened," Evelyn said.

Zach regarded the encroaching darkness. "What about tonight? Do we keep watch? I'll go first if you want."

"Everyone is to get a good night's sleep." Nate needed to work out a plan. "Tomorrow morning we start in earnest, and with any luck in a day or so we'll have our home all to ourselves again."

"How about if I set more traps before we turn in?" Zach proposed.

Nate reached up and touched the bump on his head. "No. We'll let our visitor think we've given up. Tomorrow night, when he doesn't expect it, we'll surprise him."

Zach liked the idea. It was great to be working with his father instead of behind his father's back, great that his father was relying on him, even greater that he was being treated like a man and not a boy. "I'll see to the horses and be right in," he volunteered.

"I'll help him," Lou was quick to mention.

"And I'll go light the lanterns and get the fire going," Evelyn said. Humming to herself, she pranced indoors.

Nate and Winona were alone again. They embraced, Winona rubbing her head under his chin and lightly kissing his chest. "I thank you, husband, for bending to my wishes. You have brought us all closer together."

Doubts plagued Nate, but he refrained from saying so. His decision might cost some of them their lives, and he would never forgive himself if the worst came to pass. Hard choices like these were what made parenthood so taxing, what made hair turn prematurely gray. "I just hope I did the right thing," he replied, and let it go at that.

Everyone was in fine spirits for the first time in days. Nate broke out playing cards he had bought at Bent's Fort and Winona served the last of her sweetcake. Until well past nine they relaxed and laughed and joked, merry as larks. They were having so much fun that when Winona said it was late and everyone should turn in, Evelyn protested, pleading to be allowed to stay up longer.

"You heard your mother," Nate said. "We have a big day ahead of us. So get to bed."

Zach didn't mind, since the sooner they fell asleep, the earlier they would be up the next day, and the sooner they could set to work bringing the intruder to bay. Unrolling his bedding, he spread out his blankets and crawled under them fully dressed so when morning came, he would be ready and raring to go.

The girls lay side by side, whispering and tittering, as was their habit.

Nate sat back in his chair and stretched. He was drowsy himself. The fire had burned low, but he wouldn't rekindle it until dawn. "How about you?" he asked his wife. "Are you ready to raise the roof with your snoring?"

Winona pursed her lips. Her unfortunate tendency was a constant family joke and no end of embarrassment. "I will put my pillow over my head so I do not disturb the rest of you."

"No need. We're used to it by now." Nate had never told her, but discovering she snored had been one of the major shocks of their marriage. It had simply never occurred to him women did. He'd never been permitted in his parents' bedroom, and couldn't recall ever seeing his mother asleep. Somehow or other, he'd gotten the idea women were too dainty and sweet to make any of the everyday noises men did.

"Just as I am used to your belching," Winona responded. To say nothing of the awful sound he made when he cleared his nose.

"Let's call it a day." Standing, Nate barred the door, drew the curtains over the windows, and blew out the lantern. Enough light from the fireplace illuminated the cabin for him to make his way to the bed without bumping into the furniture. He removed his shirt and moccasins but not his pants.

"Pull the blanket," Winona said.

To assure them some small degree of privacy, Nate had rigged a blanket on a pine rod so it screened the bed from the rest of the room. He would have liked to add a whole new room, but that would require more time than he had been able to spare. Lying on his back, he propped his head in his hand.

Winona removed her dress and slid under the quilt, a gift from Blue Water Woman, Shakespeare's wife. The smooth material was cool on her skin. She curled on her side and rested a cheek on her husband's broad, muscular shoulder, as content as it was possible for a woman to be. "Why are you not under the quilt also?"

Nate shrugged his free shoulder. "Too much on my mind to sleep right away. I need to think."

"Do that in the morning. Rest will refresh you, give you a new outlook on our problem."

Nate was tickled by how she was so willing to share *everything* with him, the bad along with the good. Not once in all the winters they'd been together had she ever given him cause to complain about her loyalty. She was always there for him, through thick and thin, as the old saw had it. Kissing her forehead, he said, "Have I mentioned lately how much I care for you?"

"Flatterer. I suppose you want a back rub?" By her reckoning, Winona had given him several thousand. Why he was so fond of them was as inexplicable as his need to take one of his books when he went off into the woods to heed Nature's call. Men, by their very nature, were so odd that it was a wonder women were able to get along with them at all.

"I'll spare you tonight," Nate said, idly running his fingers through her long, silken tresses.

"You must have a fever," Winona bantered.

It would simplify things if the events of the past week could be attributed to delirium, Nate mused. He could get on with his life and not live in perpetual fear for those he cared for. Mulling his options, he closed his eyes. The girls had stopped whispering, and the snap and crackle of firewood lulled him into dozing.

How much time went by, Nate couldn't say. When he woke, Winona was sound asleep, her lips fluttering against his chest. His left shoulder had a cramp, but he didn't want to move, because it might awaken her. Drowsy, he shut his eyes again, the soft down pillow cushioning his head so comfortably, he was asleep within moments.

Much later, Nate stirred and gazed dreamily at the ceiling. He had been having a sensational dream. Winona and he had gone off into the mountains alone and were living in a lean-to in a lush paradise where they bathed daily in a spectacular waterfall and spent their nights doing things they hadn't done much of since the children were born. Or not as much as Nate would like.

A log popped and sputtered. Nate debated adding wood to the fire to keep the cabin warm until morning, but he was too at ease to get up. It took a bit for the scratching to register. A steady *scritch-scritch-scritch*, like fingernails rasping across the floor. He figured it must be Evelyn or Lou, doing it in their sleep. His daughter was forever turning and tossing. She couldn't lie still for two seconds if her life depended on it.

But as the noise continued and Nate was able to pinpoint it, he realized it was coming from the front of the cabin, not the rear where the girls were. His next guess was that it must be a curious coon or porcupine, clawing at the door. The longer he listened, though, the more positive he was the sound emanated from near the counter.

A mouse was Nate's third likely candidate. Gnawing a hole through the wall, no doubt. In the morning he would check, find where it had eaten into the wood, and plug the hole up. Turning his head, he didn't give the mouse another thought. Gradually, he drifted into that fuzzy state between wakefulness and the land of Nod. Almost asleep, he realized the scratching wasn't coming from low to the ground as it would if a mouse were to blame, but from halfway up the wall.

Nate told himself he must be mistaken. Rousing, he rose onto his elbows to listen. There was no denying it. The noise *was* too high up to be made by a mouse.

A dark suspicion snapped Nate instantly alert. Carefully sliding out from under Winona, he parted the blanket. Zach breathed heavily, deep asleep. As did Lou. Evelyn was bundled in her bedding. From a shelf Nate took a pistol and padded on his bare feet to the table. The scratching persisted. Tilting his head, he ascertained exactly where it came from: the window to the left of the door.

Nate glided soundlessly to the curtain. Fashioned from a woolen Hudson's Bay Point blanket, it was heavy enough to keep out drafts and dust. Inserting a finger between the edge and the sill, he bent an eye to the crack. The night was pitch black, and from out of the blackness, at the bottom of the window, rose a small paw—or was it a hand?—capped by slightly curved claws or talons that scraped against the pane.

Dumbfounded, Nate backed to the door. He quietly removed the bar, leaned it against a chair, then slowly lifted the latch. Thumbing back the flintlock's hammer, he girded himself. Their nocturnal visitor had made one visit too many. Now he would learn who or what it was! Flinging the door inward, he sprang outside and swung toward the window. His finger began to tighten on the trigger.

Nothing was there.

Nate pivoted to either side, but the clearing was empty. Incredibly, whatever had been at the window had reached cover in the second or two it took him to show himself. Yet no living thing was that fast. He ran to the northeast corner.

Out of the cabin spilled Zach, half awake, his rifle level. "Pa? Pa?" The opening of the door had spoiled a delightful fantasy involving Louisa, him, and a picnic on Long's Peak. "What is it? What's out here?"

Without answering, Nate reversed direction and sprinted past his son to the corral. The horses were as he had seen them last, flank to flank with their backsides to the cabin. Not one was asleep, as they all should be.

Winona was next to emerge, a pistol in each hand. She had thrown a blanket over her shoulders, and the stiff breeze threatened to blow it off. Clamping her elbows against it, she moved to her mate's side. "What did you see?"

"I'm not rightly sure," Nate said. The feeling of helplessness crept over him again and to vent his anger he kicked the lowest rail. "It got clean away."

The whole family was up now. Evelyn and Lou were framed in the doorway, Lou with a flintlock, Evelyn clutching a Shoshone doll given to her by a cousin. "What was damaged this time?" the older girl inquired.

"Just my pride," Nate said bitterly. He was sick and tired of being thwarted at every turn. "It was at a window, and I let it get away."

"Let us go back in," Winona advised, anxious that in the dark the creature could jump them before they had any inkling it was there. "We frightened it off. Which is more than we have done before."

Nate didn't share her opinion. The animal, the creature—whatever in the name of creation it was—had been the one who brought them running out of the cabin in confusion and fear. The scratching at the window wasn't a random act. It had been done on purpose. Just as the ax had been taken, their tack destroyed. Nate keenly regretted permitting his family to stay with him. It still wasn't too late to make them leave, but that would require him to go back on his word.

Winona lit a lantern and placed it on the table. The girls filed to their blankets and wearily sank back down, Evelyn yawning loudly. Zach sat across from his mother, too excited to sleep. Nate barred the door and made sure the curtains were fully drawn so the skulker in the woods couldn't see in.

"I can heat some coffee," Winona said.

Nate shook his head. Coffee would keep them up for hours. Judging by the stars, it wasn't much past one, and it was best they got as much sleep as they could.

"Maybe I should keep watch, after all," Zach said. All he needed was one shot, one clear shot, right through his mother's precious glass, if need be.

"There's no need, son. It won't be back tonight," Nate said, although he felt no such certainty. Predicting what the creature would do next was as impossible as predicting a grizzly's behavior.

Zach fidgeted like a bloodhound eager to take up the hunt. "You should let me dig holes under both windows tomorrow and rig them with sharp stakes." He didn't look at Lou to see if she had overheard.

"Either that, or we'll—" Nate began, and instantly stopped, his eyes locked on the same curtain.

"Listen!" Winona exclaimed.

Claws were scratching on the pane again.

Chapter Seven

Zach King never thought he would live to see the day when anyone or anything got the better of his father. But earlier, when he'd heard the door being opened and had rushed outside, he'd seen a look on his father's face he'd never seen before. A look of utter, baffled helplessness. And he'd remembered the statement his father had made to his mother, in a voice choked with anguish: *"I can't stop it."*

That statement repeated itself over and over in Zach's head after he turned in. He couldn't stop thinking about how terrified his father sounded. The great Grizzly Killer, the man reputed to never know fear, was experiencing it now. And that made Zach mad, boiling mad at the creature that had caused his father the despair. An unquenchable thirst for revenge filled him.

So when the scratching resumed, Zach was out of his chair and at the window before anyone else. With the barrel of his rifle he swept the heavy curtain aside, then sighted down it at a shape just outside. A face suddenly pressed against the pane, a demonic, grinning, gargoyle face, all hair and teeth and glowing red eyes, arrogantly staring up at him, almost as if defying him to pull the trigger.

Zach hesitated. He couldn't help himself. The thing was so eerily inhuman, its devilish features so savage, he was too startled to shoot. He gaped, and the creature's cruel grin widened.

Winona was almost to her son's side, her arm outflung. Not to fire her pistol, but to grab his rifle. "Not through the glass!" Her cherished glass, which would take a year to replace, if, in fact, they were able to have a new pane sent at all. "Please, son! No!"

Her cry snapped Zach from his daze, and he fixed the front bead squarely between the creature's eyes. But his moment of delay proved costly. The thing dropped from sight. Zach leaned down to try to catch a glimpse of it and saw not one but *two* dwarfish figures scuttling toward the forest with blinding speed. In a span of heartbeats they were in the vegetation.

Winona grabbed the Hawken, even though she saw he wasn't going to fire. "What did you see?" she asked. "What does it look like?"

They both felt a rush of cool air and turned. The door was wide open.

Nate King had no intention of letting the thing get away. He ran outside and saw a short dark shape sprinting into the woods. Immediately, he gave chase. Ignoring a shout from his wife, he declared, "Not again!" and was in among the trees in time to spot his quarry moving briskly to the northeast.

Shirtless and shoeless, armed with only a pistol, Nate raced after it. He had to exert himself to his fullest to keep it in sight, glimpsing it now and again as it crossed open spots.

Nate couldn't get over how small it was, no higher than his knees. He realized it must have been standing on something in order to reach the cabin window, which was five feet off the ground. In the stygian veil of night, Nate couldn't distinguish much else about it. The only animal he could think of that its silhouette even remotely resembled was a bear cub. Then the creature came to a starlit clearing and paused to look back. Dumbfounded, Nate inadvertently slowed.

It stood erect on two legs, not four. The head, the body, the limbs were similar to those of a human but were decidedly unhuman. The proportions were all wrong, the head just a bit too big, the torso a bit too thin, the arms longer than the legs. To call the face hideous did not do it justice. It radiated pure evil, accented by gleaming bloodred eyes. It was a creature ripped from a demented nightmare, yet it was undeniably real.

In New York City, Nate had seen dwarfs and midgets. The thing in the starlight was about the same size but was as different from them as the moon from the sun. It was as if all the worst traits and qualities ever imagined had been given physical form. As if all that was wicked had been lent flesh and sinew.

Nate raised his pistol. He had no qualms about killing something so vile. Indeed, he yearned to slay the fiend. He felt a strange compulsion to blot it from existence, a deep-rooted urge to wipe it from the earth.

But it wasn't meant to be.

Whirling, the creature faded into the undergrowth. Nate pursued it, wincing whenever he trod on sharp twigs and stones. His left foot had been cut and he was bleeding, but he refused to turn back. Not now, not when he could end his family's ordeal and make their valley safe to live in once again.

On and on Nate sprinted. Far off, Zach was shouting, wanting to know where he was, but Nate didn't reply. This was his to do, and his alone. He hurtled a log, sped through a barrier of pine boughs, and reached a clearing. Advancing another dozen steps, Nate sought the creature but couldn't spot it.

"No!" To have been so close, then to lose it, filled Nate with wrath. He was breathing heavily and had to will himself to stay calm, to not give his frustration free rein. His cut foot stung terribly.

Zach was still bawling his name. Cupping a hand to his mouth, Nate turned to reply—the yell dying in his throat when he saw the creature *behind* him, at the edge of the clearing, down on all fours and licking the grass. Stunned, Nate just stood there. He couldn't make any sense out of what it was doing.

Moist trickling along his sole flooded Nate with insight and horror. *The thing is licking up drops of blood!* As if it could read his thoughts, it uncurled, grinning. In pure reflex Nate jerked the pistol up and out, but the creature spun and executed an extraordinary leap into the trees. Nate ran forward to get a shot off and saw only a dark mass of foliage.

"Pa! Pa! Where are you?"

His son was much closer.

"Here!" Nate acknowledged. "I'm over here! Be careful! The thing is nearby!"

Zach didn't care. Overcome by worry, he charged through the brush. His relief at finding his father unharmed knew no bounds, which was in itself disturbing. There had been a time when he believed his pa was invincible. "Where did they go?"

"They?"

"There are two of those vermin."

"Two?" Nate stopped scouring the branches and boles. "Are you sure? I saw only one of them."

"As I live and breathe," Zach vowed. "Crazy as it sounds, I figure one was standing on the shoulders of the other when they were at the window. What are they, Pa? Where do they come from?"

Nate would give a parfleche full of gold to know. But worthy of more urgent consideration was another aspect. Namely, where there were two, might there not be more?

Zach didn't rate it wise of them to linger. They had one gun apiece and no spare ammunition. "We sure did run a far piece," he commented. "Must be pretty near a mile. Shouldn't we head back and get our powder horns and bullets?"

"I suppose." Nate was loath to give up.

"The second one must not have come the same way you did, or you'd have seen it," Zach mentioned. "I wonder where it got to."

Mountain Nightmare

The riddle was apparently solved by the popping of gunfire from somewhere near the cabin.

As her husband dashed into the pines, Winona King turned to her son and gave him a push. "Go help your father, Stalking Coyote! Cover his back! And be careful!"

Given her mate's current state of mind, Winona was more apprehensive than she would normally be for his safety. He was a mighty fighter and had counted many coup, but even the best of warriors could be brought low by self-doubt. She'd seen it happen with her own eyes.

Once a Shoshone by the name of Wiskin, or Cut Hair, had earned great distinction in battle. Proudly hung in his lodge were the scalps of Crows, Dakotas, and Arapahos. At all the councils his judgment in matters related to war had been considered final and complete. He was well on his way to becoming leader of the entire tribe.

Then one day the unthinkable occurred. Piegans raided the village and tried to steal the horse herd. The Shoshones rallied and resisted, Wiskin leading the counterattack. He was confronted by the leader of the Piegan war party, who rushed forward brandishing a war club.

Wiskin, who held a bow, swiftly drew the string back and sent a glittering shaft straight at the Piegan's heart. But he missed.

Later, other warriors would say that it was because Wiskin rushed his shot. They told him it didn't matter. The Shoshones had repulsed the invaders with no loss of life and recovered all but four of the stolen horses. No one faulted Wiskin for the miss.

No one except Wiskin himself. He started to doubt his ability, to think he was not the warrior he should be. With bow, lance, and club he practiced hour after hour, day after day, honing his skill. Twenty times he'd hit a target dead center with an arrow, but if, on the twenty-first, he missed by the breadth of an otter's whisker, he would say that was proof he was not the man he had once been.

His family tried to convince him otherwise. His friends insisted he was acting foolish. Wisken wouldn't listen to them. He closed his ears to all but his own doubt.

Then one day a campaign was mounted against the Crows, who had been making bold forays into Shoshone territory. Wiskin joined a war party and in pitched combat was slain. Those who saw his end reported that he froze when attacked, that he'd nocked a shaft and taken aim and then stood quaking as a tall Crow bore down on him and transfixed his chest with a lance.

If it could happen to Wiskin, it could happen to Nate. Winona intended to ensure it didn't. She waited until the crackling of vegetation dwindled, then she moved to the doorway, where her youngest and her future daughter-in-law waited.

"Again?" Lou said. She had just drifted off when the commotion erupted. Sleep clung to her like cobwebs but didn't dull the dismay she felt at her betrothed vanishing into the woods.

"We'll wait for them inside," Winona directed.

"I'd rather wait on the roof, Ma," Evelyn said, smothering a yawn. She had always loved to climb up there and play. "We'll see them from a long way off."

"Not in the dark." Winona ushered the pair indoors. After brief consideration she barred the door, then stepped to the left window and opened the curtains. "The two of you can go back to bed if you want."

"We'd only be woke up again," Lou said. In reality, she couldn't sleep anyway, not until Zach was safe.

Evelyn plopped into a chair. "I'd like some tea, Ma, if you don't mind. The mint kind. It always helps calm me."

"Hot tea, right away," Winona said. It would give her something to do, something to take her mind off her husband and her son. The leaves were in a canister in a high cupboard, the teapot under the counter. From a bucket refilled twice daily at the lake, she ladled enough water to fill it.

"Did you see what it was?" Lou asked. She hadn't, and she was dying to find out.

"No. It was gone when I ran out," Winona responded. "It could have been a porcupine for all I know."

Snickering, Evelyn said, "Porcupines don't drag axes off, Ma. Maybe it was that little critter I saw today in the woods—" She caught herself, but it was too late. The lack of sleep had made her careless.

Winona whipped around. "Today, when you were in the trees? What little animal? You mentioned none to me."

Evelyn placed her elbows on the table and propped her chin in her hands. She was in for it now. "I didn't think it was important. I never did find out what it was. A coon, maybe, but I never heard of a coon with shiny eyeballs."

"Eyes do not glow in the daytime," Winona said. At night they did, as she had witnessed on many occasions. No sooner did she have the thought than she glanced at the window and was riveted by a pair of scarlet eyes peering in over the sill. Startled, she recoiled, nearly dropping the teapot.

"What's wrong, Mrs. King?" Lou asked, looking in the same direction. "Land sakes!" She darted to the door and began to lift the bar.

"No!" Winona ran over and grabbed an end. "Don't go out there!"

Lou kept attempting to lift it. "What's gotten into you? We have to find out what it is, don't we? I have my pistol. I'll be safe enough."

"No, you won't!" Winona cried. More softly, almost to herself, she said, "May Apo preserve us, I know what it is!" *The eyes! The red eyes, just as in the legends!* Her daughter's stumbling on the "little man," the tack, everything now made sense, and in her heart of hearts Winona was gripped by frigid fear.

"You do?" In her surprise, Lou stopped lifting the bar, which was a few inches above the pair of stout upright braces designed to hold it in place. "What is it?"

Before Winona could say, the door was struck a resounding blow. Lou jumped back, dropping her end of the bar, and pointed her flintlock.

"Ma!" Evelyn screeched.

Another blow thundered, the door seeming to bend inward from

97

the impact. Winona tried to shove the bar into place, but it became stuck. "Quickly! Help me! It's trying to break in!" Once it did, the three of them didn't stand a chance. There was no other way out. Her home, the cabin of which she had grown so fond, would become a death trap.

Lou had been afraid many times before. Notably when her ma died on the trek west, when her pa was slain by hostiles, and when a grizzly almost killed Zach and her. But never *this* afraid, never so petrified her limbs wouldn't move and her breath caught in her throat. She wanted to help Winona, to do as she was bid, but her body wouldn't obey her will.

"What are you waiting for?" Winona had raised the bar a trifle but not high enough, and as she sought to force it into place the door shook to another tremendous crash. "Please, Lou! Before it's too late!"

Evelyn was gripping the table as if it, too, were being assaulted, and she had to cling to it for dear life. Seeing her mother's plight, she slid off the chair and grasped the older girl's wrist. "Lou? Lou? What's wrong?"

The contact shattered the spell that held Lou motionless and speechless. "Out of the way, Mrs. King! I'll shoot right through the wood!"

"No! It will do no good! Help me!"

Springing, Lou grabbed her end of the bar and assisted Winona in shoving it down behind the braces.

None too soon. The hardest blow yet slammed into the door, almost tearing it from its hinges. Had the bar not been in place, they would have been at their attacker's mercy.

"What do we do, Ma?" Evelyn bawled. She was striving her utmost to be brave, but her knees were shaking and a swarm of butterflies was loose in her stomach.

"The guns!" Winona said. "Collect all the guns and put them on the table!" Each of them had a rifle, including Evelyn, and Nate had a spare in case it was needed in an emergency. Zach had taken his with him, but that left five, plus plenty of pistols.

Both girls scurried to different corners. Winona snatched her pistol from the counter and steadied herself. Every shot must count. Legend had it that arrows and lances were of no use except at close range, but firearms hadn't been invented when the Kogohues, Pohogues, and Agaidukas drove the NunumBi into the farthermost recesses of the mountains. Maybe, Winona hoped, guns would be effective where the traditional weapons of her people were not.

"Listen!" Evelyn said. "It's stopped!"

The pounding on the door had ceased. In the dreadful silence Winona could hear the two girls panting.

Louisa was toting three rifles at once. "Do you reckon it went away, Mrs. King?" she anxiously asked.

All three of them spun when the left window dissolved in a spray of glass. A rock the size of a melon thumped onto the floor and rolled to a stop near the bed. Simultaneously, an elfin figure materialized, perched on the sill, claws digging into the walls for support.

Evelyn screamed and stumbled backward in blind panic. "It's one of the little men I saw!"

Winona pointed her pistol. For a split second all the tales she had heard about the dreaded NunumBi gave her pause. No one could defy them. No one could stand up to them and live. Whoever encountered one was as good as dead. But her daughter was in imminent peril, and her motherly instinct was to do whatever it took to remove that peril. So she fired, the flintlock belching smoke and lead.

The ball caught the creature in the chest. It was hurled into the dark as if kicked by a mule, tumbling head over heels.

"You got it, Ma!" Evelyn whooped. "You killed it!"

Winona wasn't so sure. Dropping the pistol on the table, she exchanged it for a Hawken. Their guns were always kept loaded, so all she had to do was palm back the hammer. Her future daughter-in-law was gawking at the shattered window, the rifles she carried forgotten. "Louisa! It might return! Be ready!"

Lou absently nodded and deposited the long guns on the table. What she had just seen stunned her. It defied every belief she

David Thompson

held. It flew in the face of all she had been told about the world. It was contrary to all that was and all that should be. Such things simply couldn't exist. Yet she'd beheld it with her own eyes!

"Arm yourself!" Winona commanded.

Mechanically, Lou picked up a rifle. She felt she must be dreaming, that this couldn't possibly be happening, that if she pinched herself she would sit up in her blankets and laugh at her silliness.

Without warning, another terrific crash resounded. Another rock had been thrown, through the other window. The pane broke into fragments, which rained onto the floor.

Winona swiveled. Her shot hadn't slain it, and now the NunumBi wouldn't rest until all of them were worm food. "Aim at the head!" she instructed, since the shot to the chest had proven ineffective.

Evelyn had retreated clear to her bedding and was bending to hide under the covers. The sight of her mother, so grim, so determined, wreathed in tendrils of acrid gunsmoke and ready to sell her life if need be in their defense, caused her to cast the blanket down. *What was she doing? She was a King, and Kings weren't cowards! Her pa would be ashamed if he learned how she was acting!* Clutching her pistol, she moved toward her mother's side. "I'm with you, Ma."

Distracted, Winona glanced over a shoulder. "No! Stay back!" Movement out of the corner of her eye alerted her to her mistake, and she faced the window again just as another rock sailed through. She leaped aside. It smacked onto the table, skidded off, and wound up by the rocking chair.

Lou laughed nervously. "That thing isn't very smart, is it? The window is already broken."

Suddenly rocks began flying through both windows, big, jagged rocks that could maim or cripple, one after the other without letup. The barrage drove Winona away from the table and forced Lou to skip rearward.

That so many were being thrown at the same time led Winona to an inescapable conclusion: There was more than one of the horrid brutes out there. Which fit with the legend. The NunumBi never roved singly, always in pairs or packs.

Changing positions hadn't helped. Rocks were being thrown at the center of the room as well as to both sides, some high, some low, crashing against furniture, against the walls, the floor. The cupboard was open, and one struck a pile of plates. Another broke a glass on the counter.

Winona dodged one, saw another fly toward Lou, and hollered, "Look out!"

Louisa wasn't caught flatfooted. Pivoting, she narrowly escaped injury. It dawned on her that the constant pelting was slowly but inevitably driving them farther and farther from the windows. Once they'd been driven far enough, their attackers could rush in unopposed. Dashing to the right wall, she sidled toward the front.

"What are you doing?" Winona asked, fearful the girl had lost her senses. Panic in combat was fatal. Shoshone warriors were taught that losing one's head led to losing one's hair. It was critical to always stay calm, be rational, think things through.

Lou was almost close enough to see over the sill when rocks flew straight at her, thick and furious. The creatures knew what she was attempting to do. She ducked, but a deluge of stony projectiles smashed into the wall and rained down, gouging and scraping her shoulders, her lower back. One glanced off her brow, drawing blood.

"Get away from there!" Winona yelled.

Turning to do just that, Lou winced when a rock jarred her left arm so severely, her arm went numb. She leaned against the wall and willed her fingers to move, but they wouldn't.

Winona headed across the room to help. More rocks, streaming in through the other window, prevented her. One smashed into her ribs, another into her shin. How the monsters could see what she was doing, she didn't know. She was driven back. In great pain, bleeding from her leg, she racked her brain for a means of driving the creatures off.

Evelyn had hung back, as her mother told her to do. But now, with her ma and Lou pinned down, she rushed to their aid.

"Don't!" Winona cried, frantically waving her off. Some of the rocks were big enough to crush her daughter's skull.

But Evelyn didn't heed. She ran toward her mother, railing at their tormentors, "Let her be! Let her be!" Amazingly, as she came near, the stream of rocks coming in the left window abruptly stopped.

Not those being thrown through the right window, though. Louisa was on her knees, rocks raining around her like cannonballs. With no regard for her own safety, Evelyn veered toward the older girl. Almost instantly, the barrage on that side ended. Evelyn reached Lou, slid an arm under hers, and boosted Louisa upward. "Come on! Over to my ma!"

Winona covered the windows, swinging her rifle from one to the other, primed to shoot if so much as a claw appeared. As the girls sank down beside her, she moved in front of them, screening them with her own body.

"Are they gone, Ma?" Evelyn asked. "Please say they're gone!"

"I doubt it," Winona said. The NunumBi were as tenacious as they were vicious. They never gave up. Once they picked a victim, they didn't rest until their enemy was destroyed.

"Listen!" Lou said. Her arm was tingling with pain, but she could lift her rifle high enough to shoot.

Evelyn's hands were shaking. "What is it?"

Winona heard the sounds, too. Loud crashing in the woods. She imagined the creatures breaking limbs and tearing out brush, but for what purpose? There was a commotion of some sort, then another heavy blow to the door. Winona had had enough. She fixed her sights on the center of the door and squeezed the trigger at the very moment it was flung inward and her husband burst into the cabin.

Chapter Eight

Fear lent Nate King speed he'd never tapped. Fear his wife and the girls were under attack. Fear he'd blundered badly in running off, in leaving them alone, and that they would pay for his stupidity with their lives.

Nothing stood in Nate's way. He crashed through thickets. He barreled through dense pines. Limbs that snagged him were broken in half or ripped off. He was a bull gone amok, plowing through anything and everything.

Zach had never witnessed his father in the grip of a berserk fury. It was all Zach could do to keep him in sight. Several times he'd hollered for his father to slow down, but he might as well have been yelling at the stars. Now he tried again.

"Pa! Wait for me!"

Nate would have liked to but couldn't, not when every precious second was so vital, not when any delay might spell doom for Winona and the girls. "Do the best you can, son," he answered on the fly.

By now Nate's eyes were so adjusted to the dark that two yellow squares ahead stood out like blazing torches. It was lantern light, spilling from the cabin's windows. Ordinarily, their thick curtains would keep all but a pale glow from showing. So either Winona had opened them . . . or they had been torn off.

The breeze brought the acrid odor of gunsmoke, fueling Nate's terror. Arriving at the the clearing, he flew across it without breaking stride, thankful no bodies littered the grass. A voice from inside, his daughter's, reached him, louder than it should be, and he realized the glass panes were gone, that the windows had been shattered. Lowering a shoulder, he rammed into the door, pumping the latch as he did and spilling over the threshold.

Nate saw Winona, saw the muzzle of her rifle trained on him, but he couldn't stop. Which was just as well. His momentum carried him past the door at the exact instant her rifle boomed. Wood splintered, showering slivers, but he had eyes only for his wife, daughter, and Lou. ''You're safe!''

Winona thought her heart had stopped. Snapping the rifle down, she sagged against the wall, horrified she had almost killed the man she loved. When he embraced her, she clung to him, as weak as a newborn.

Outside, Zach had just come to the clearing when the blast thundered. Figuring his father was shooting at one of the creatures, he let loose with a piercing Shoshone war whoop and raced on in to join the fray.

Zach stopped short in surprise. His parents were hugging. His sister had her arms around their father's leg and was quietly sobbing. Beyond them, slumped against the wall, was Lou. Zach had been so engrossed in overtaking his pa that he hadn't really considered she might be harmed. On beholding her doubled over, wincing as she lifted an arm, his chest constricted. He was to her in one leap, sweeping her up and pressing her close. ''Are you all right?''

''I am now,'' Lou said.

Zach was counting on spending the rest of his days with her. It never occurred to him she might die. He'd taken it for granted she would live to a fine old age, as if their love bestowed immunity from death. But it didn't. They were mortal like everyone else. She might live fifty years or die the very next day. The idea of life without her was bleak and unappealing; he'd rather die himself.

Lou was watching the doorway and windows, afraid the attack would be renewed. "Did you see them? Those awful eyes? I've never been so scared in my life."

"You're safe now," Zach said.

Nate, overhearing, raised his head to survey the damage. His son should do the same, he thought. Then Zach would appreciate how wrong he was.

Fist-size rocks were everywhere. The walls, the floor, the table and chairs were all scarred, dented, and scraped. Broken glass lay in glittering pieces, and shattered dishes covered the counter. Small clouds of gunsmoke had yet to disperse. It looked as if a war had been waged.

"I wish you'd been here, Pa," Evelyn said, sniffling. "Those things wouldn't have dared try to get us."

Her remark sparked a troubling question. Had the creatures deliberately lured him off? Nate wondered. Exactly how intelligent, how clever, were they? "Tell me everything," he said, steering Winona to the table so she could sit, "after Zach and I take a few precautions." The first step was to board up the windows, but to do that they needed wood from the spare room at the rear. Nate shared his plan and turned to go.

"No!" Winona said, grabbing his wrist. "You must stay here with us until daylight. Only then will it be safe."

Rarely did she dispute him. Nate held her hands, kissed her knuckles. "It has to be done. I won't take long."

Winona gripped his wrist. "Please don't. They are NunumBi, the dwarfs my people have told you about. They can see in the dark, like cats. But they go below ground during the day. Wait until morning, husband, I beg you."

Nate could count the number of times his wife had pleaded so desperately on one finger. He was inclined to say she must be mistaken, that the NunumBi were no more than figments of Shoshone myth, but after what had transpired, after what he had seen, he couldn't deny the truth.

"Please."

Undecided, Nate studied the others. Tears streamed down Evelyn's cheeks and her lips were trembling. Louisa appeared to be in mild shock. "I'll stay." He suggested she take the girls to the back of the cabin. Then, with Zach lending a hand, he barred the door and propped a chair against it, pulled the heavy curtains closed, and spread pots and pans under both windows.

Meanwhile, Winona had bundled Evelyn and Lou in blankets and bid them try to sleep. She hunkered in front of the fireplace, rekindling the flames.

Nate positioned the rocking chair near her but facing the windows, and sat with his Hawken across his thighs. They swapped accounts, Nate aghast at the trial she had endured. A few aspects puzzled him. Why, for instance, had the NunumBi been content to throw rocks when a concerted rush might have overwhelmed Winona and the girls? Was it because the creatures were afraid of bright light, as the Shoshones believed? There had been a lantern on the table the whole time. But about that lantern—why didn't the creatures simply hit it with a rock? It was almost as if the NunumBi wanted Winona and the others to see what was happening, almost as if the whole attack had been staged to scare them rather than harm them. As if the dwarfs took great delight in toying with their victims.

Another thing, Nate reflected. How many creatures were there? The one that led him into the woods couldn't possibly have participated in the attack. Zach swore he'd seen two, but based on what Winona said, there had to have been three or four more.

So many questions! Nate mused. Where had the creatures come from? Why had they appeared now, after so many years? Why were they so hostile? Was it as the Shoshones believed, that the NunumBi were by their very nature evil and bloodthirsty? Or was there more to it?

The only thing Nate knew beyond a shadow of a doubt was that he must spirit his family away from there. At dawn they would pack up, throw saddles on their mounts, and be gone before the sun cleared the eastern mountains. He would conduct them to the village of Winona's uncle, leave them there for safekeeping, and hasten to Shakespeare McNair's. His mentor was one of the few who wouldn't think his wits had crumbled to dust, who would help him drive the NunumBi back into whatever pit spawned them. He could also count on Scott Kendall and Simon Ward. Maybe one or two others.

"Husband?"

Nate hadn't realized his wife was talking to him. "Sorry," he said. "I was thinking about what to do."

"What else? We will fight for our home. All of us, together. Just as we discussed."

"That was before we knew what we were up against," Nate said, gesturing. "You can't expect me to expose the rest of you to more of this? We're leaving. Let the NunumBi think they've won. In a couple of weeks Shakespeare and I will show them how wrong they are."

Winona put down the poker and slid next to him. Affectionately caressing his cheek, she said softly, "You gave your word."

"So?"

Winona continued to caress him.

"So?" Nate repeated. Her expression was an eloquent rebuke. "You're not holding me too it, are you?"

"What have you always said about a person who doesn't keep it?"

Nate King kicked the floor. He kicked the chair. He kicked the wall. He muttered. He glowered. At length his shoulders slumped and he declared gruffly, "Damn me for being an idiot."

Toward dawn Nate dozed off and was ashamed for his lapse. The merry chirping of a robin snapped his head up. Befuddled, he heaved out of the rocking chair, vigorously shaking his head to clear it. Winona was curled up in a buffalo robe beside the fireplace. Zach, Evelyn, and Lou were deep in slumber.

Nate moved stiffly to the left window and carefully moved the

107

curtain. The sun hadn't risen yet but would soon. Daylight meant an end to their nightmare, at least until sunset. He had twelve hours in which to prepare, and he intended to make the most of every minute.

Quietly opening the door, Nate slipped outside. The brisk morning air helped invigorate him. With the Hawken cocked he made a circuit of the cabin and the corral. The horses hadn't been molested and everything else was as it should be.

A golden arch to the east was giving birth to the new day. Nate inhaled deeply, glad to be alive and profoundly thankful his family had not been harmed. His stomach growled, reminding him it was time for breakfast, but rather than wake Winona he went to the spare room at the rear and brought out all his traps, his two shovels, a rope, an ax, and other implements.

Now that Nate knew the nature of the enemy his outlook had changed. Gone was the nagging sense of hopelessness that had sapped his will and crushed his spirit. Uncertainty was like acid, eating at a person's vitals. He now had the information he needed to wage war on his terms, not the NunumBis'.

To that end, Nate began by setting all his beaver traps. His son had held the right idea all along—only, they had to account for the fact they were dealing with creatures much smarter than the average painter or bear. They had to be as devious as the dwarfs, as crafty as if they were setting the traps for men instead of beasts.

Nate rigged snares next to each beaver trap. He dug pits and embedded stakes at the bottom but didn't cover them quite well enough to hide them, then dug adjacent pits and used all his skill to conceal the second ones. He set deadfalls, lots of deadfalls, log deadfalls and boulder deadfalls, deadfalls with branches for triggers and more elaborate ones with cord. He bent two saplings crosswise, linking them by rope, the other end a loop hidden by high grass. He broke off straight limbs, sharpened them to points, and arranged trip ropes so that whatever blundered into one was in for an unpleasant surprise.

Wrapped in his work, Nate lost track of time. It was the middle of the morning when he looked up from a hook snare he had just set and saw his wife coming toward him. Her hair was disheveled and she was yawning, the robe still over her shoulders.

"Why did you let me sleep so late?" Winona asked. She couldn't remember the last time she had slept past sunrise. It smacked of laziness, and among her people sloth was as frowned upon as speaking with two tongues.

"You needed the rest," Nate said, standing. "Are the others up?"

"Not yet, but Zach was stirring." Winona stared at the snare, then at a deadfall close to it. "I see you have been busy."

"Very," Nate acknowledged. "Tonight those bastards won't get off so easy."

The venom in his tone disturbed Winona. One trait of his she most admired was his ability to stay levelheaded in a crisis. "You are taking this very personal, husband."

"You're damn right I am." Nate pointed at the windows. "I don't care what these things are. I don't care if they're as old as time itself. They've violated our home. They've threatened you and the kids. For that, they deserve to die."

"They are hard to kill," Winona observed. "My people have always feared them more than any other. More than the giants, more than the thunderbirds."

"The Shoshones beat them once. We can do the same." Nate reclaimed his rifle, which he'd leaned against an oak.

"How? There are only four of us. Five, if you count Blue Flower."

"We'll find a way." Nate hooked an arm through hers and they strolled toward the cabin. "I want all our lanterns filled and ready for use. I want a dozen torches made. Have the girls gather firewood and fill the bin to overflowing. And have Zach load every gun."

"You have this all thought out."

Nate had been plotting as he worked. "We'll need the buckets filled with water. The water skins, too. And whatever else you have handy. Later today we'll board up the windows."

David Thompson

Winona stopped. "Is that wise? How will we fight back? Or escape if they break in?"

"You'll see," was all Nate would say.

Louisa May Clark slid the strap to a full water skin over her left shoulder and grunted. "Your folks sure are working us to death. If I have to tote one more of these, my arms will fall off."

Evelyn sighed. "I know what you mean. We have enough water to last a year. We don't need any more." She lifted the bucket she had just filled for the third time.

"Your pa seems to think so. I've never seen him work so hard. All that brush he gathered. And those branches. What do you reckon he has in mind?"

"I asked him. But all he did was kiss me on the nose and tell me to keep busy." Evelyn walked toward the trail and her waiting brother. "If I was any busier, I'd keel over from being too tired to take a step."

"Will you two quit your jabbering and hurry it up?" Zach called out. "Pa and I have a lot to do before nightfall."

"My, my. Isn't he grumpy?" Evelyn said, giggling.

Lou didn't find it quite so humorous. Zach had been irritable all day. Why, she couldn't guess. She had been meaning to ask him, so as they trudged homeward with him bringing up the rear for protection, she did.

"Me, irritable? I don't know what you're talking about."

Men, Lou had found, could be almost as pigheaded as the real article. They had a bothersome practice of refusing to admit what was plain to everyone else. Especially when it applied to them. Like horses with blinders on, they saw only what they wanted to see. "You've been as grumpy as a badger with a thorn in its paw," she countered. "What's wrong?"

Zach pondered whether to say. He was upset because of her. Or, rather, because he'd not been there when she needed him. All day the image of her doubled over in pain had plagued him, reminding him she had nearly died, reminding him he'd almost lost the girl he loved more than life itself. Rather than go into all

110

of that, he simply said, "I don't want to lose you."

"Is that what has you out of sorts?" Lou smiled at the depth of his devotion. *How sweet of him.* "You won't. So quit fretting."

Zach didn't share her optimism. The attack had taught him an important lesson. Nothing in life was ironclad. No one knew from one day to the next whether they'd be alive to greet the next sunrise. If he desired to live to a nice old age with Lou at his side—and he desired nothing more—he must watch over her every waking moment.

"Now that I've thought about it," Lou said, trying to put him at ease, "I don't think the NunumBi were trying to kill us last night. They could have, easily. But they were content to chuck rocks."

"Any one of which could have split your noggin," Zach said. The creatures had a lot to answer for, and if his pa and he had anything to say about it, they would. "Don't make them out to be something they're not. They like to torment folks. They enjoy it."

"Has anyone ever stopped to wonder why? Have they always hated humans? Or is there a reason they do what they do?"

"Who cares?" Zach branded the issue as so much nonsense. "When a grizzly is trying to eat someone, the person doesn't ask why. When a panther is trying to claw a trapper to shreds, he doesn't ask why. Everyone knows. It's what they do, how they are, their nature. The same with the NunumBi."

"You can't say that for sure," Lou argued. "Has anyone ever tried to communicate with them? Get them to change? My ma used to say that the only way to make friends is to be friendly."

Zach envisioned her offering a hand in friendship to one of the savage little creatures and having it bitten clean off. "And my pa likes to say that you can't throw a saddle on a buffalo. Some things just can't be done, and no amount of wishful thinking will make them come true."

"You never know until you try," Lou declared, getting in the last word.

Evelyn had been listening with half an ear. "I'll never try, I

David Thompson

can tell you that right now. I'd as soon spoon-feed a wolverine."

Zach laughed heartily. Every now and then his sister was actually funny. "Or try to sneak up on a skunk."

"Remember when Blue Feather tried?" Evelyn said. "He stunk to high heaven for a whole moon."

Zach's laughter swelled. "His parents wouldn't let him sleep in the lodge even when it rained."

"Oh, the poor child," Lou said.

"Child?" Now both brother and sister cackled. "Blue Feather was twenty-two," Zach said. "Afterward, everyone called him Smells Bad. They still do."

"You wouldn't believe it was so hilarious if it had happened to you," Lou mentioned.

Zach's mirth died. Did she honestly and truly belive he was dumb enough to pull a boneheaded stunt like that? Before he could ask they arrived at the clearing and he spied his father by the storage room, bent over something he couldn't quite make out. "Talk to you later."

Nate King had taken every precaution he could think of, but he worried there was one or two he'd overlooked. A battle was about to be waged, a fierce battle for his family's right to go on calling the valley their home, and he had to avail himself of every opportunity to punish the NunumBi for their transgressions. He had a whole sequence of surprises set up. Whether they would work, whether he'd succeed in driving the creatures off, remained to be seen.

Hearing his son approach, Nate looked up. It warmed his heart, how they had all pitched in to do what had to be done. Everyone realized what was at stake. "Are they done with the water?"

"Every water skin, every pot, every pan is filled to the brim," Zach reported. "Although why we need so much is beyond me, Pa."

"We're fighting fire with fire," Nate said. "And I don't want our cabin to burn down in the process."

Zach nodded at the keg of black powder his father had. "What

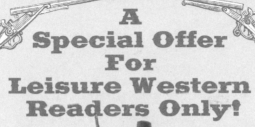

GET YOUR 4 FREE* BOOKS NOW— A VALUE BETWEEN $16 AND $20

Mail the Free* Book Certificate Today!

FREE* BOOKS CERTIFICATE!

YES! I want to subscribe to the Leisure Western Book Club. Please send me my 4 FREE* BOOKS. Then, each month, I'll receive the four newest Leisure Western Selections to preview FREE* for 10 days. If I decide to keep them, I will pay the Special Member's Only discounted price of just $3.36 each, a total of $13.44 ($14.50 US in Canada). This saves me between $3 and $6 off the bookstore price. There are no shipping, handling or other charges.* There is no minimum number of books I must buy and I may cancel the program at any time. In any case, the 4 FREE* BOOKS are mine to keep—at a value of between $17 and $20!

*In Canada, add $5.00 Canadian shipping and handling per order for first shipment. For all subsequent shipments to Canada the cost of membership in the Book Club is $14.50 US, which includes $7.50 shipping and handling per month. All payments must be made in US currency.

Name _____

Address _____

City_____ State_____ Country_____

Zip_____ Telephone_____

Tear here and mail your FREE* book card today!

Get Four Books Totally F R E E* – A Value between $16 and $20

Tear here and mail your FREE* book card today!

PLEASE RUSH
MY FOUR FREE*
BOOKS TO ME
RIGHT AWAY!

LeisureWestern Book Club
P.O. Box 6613
Edison, NJ 08818-6613

are you fixing to do with that? Fill all the powder horns?''

"Already done." Nate tapped a strip of cloth he had wedged into a hole in the top. "I've inserted a fuse." Holding the keg in the crook of an arm, he rose. "This is our defense of last resort, son. Remember it in case anything happens to me."

"Nothing will," Zach said, then realized he was being as unduly optimistic as Lou.

Nate halted and placed a brawny hand on his son's shoulder. "However this night turns out, I'm trusting in you to see your mother and the girls are safe. I can't fight the NunumBi and watch over the others, too."

"You don't expect me to sit this fight out?" Zach asked, appalled. Here he thought his father was beginning to treat him as a man, as a full-fledged warrior.

"No, I don't," Nate conceded. Nor did he want Zach to rashly get himself slain. In the frenzy of kill-or-be-killed mistakes were often made, mistakes that proved fatal. Nate had no choice but to let his son take part, but he would do so in a way that reduced the risk of Zach being killed. "I do expect you to do exactly as I say, when I say it. No sass. No quarreling. Agreed?"

"Sure, Pa." Zach puffed out his chest in pride. "You can depend on me. I won't let you down." He'd gladly sacrifice his own life, should it be necessary, to save his family and fiancée.

Nate passed a deadfall situated under a low evergreen. It consisted of a hefty boulder tilted to fall when the brace was yanked on. A jiggle or two was all it would take, although he doubted the NunumBi would trigger it. They were too intelligent. But they might choose to examine how it had been set up, and if they did, his other little surprise would be sprung.

In front of the cabin Nate paused to survey his handiwork. The piles of dry brush along the perimeter of the clearing stood out like proverbial sore thumbs. As did the belt of branches strewn from north to south midway between the vegetation and the cabin. The NunumBi were bound to divine why he had done it and shy away. Then again, the creatures were arrogant. They liked to toy with humans, treating people like people treated lesser animals, a flaw that might prove to be their undoing.

"Do you think they'll tell stories about this, Pa?" Zach inquired. "The Shoshones, that is?"

Had Nate heard correctly? Here they were, preparing for the struggle of their lives, and all his oldest cared about was how much fame they would reap? "Live through it and we'll find out."

"They might, you know. Like they tell about Coyote and his brother Wolf and Jackrabbit. A hundred years from now, when the Shoshones gather around a winter's campfire, our tale will be told and retold."

Nate looked at his son. "You're serious?" He'd long been aware of Zach's dream of one day becoming a warrior of great renown, but this went far beyond that.

"Don't you want to be remembered? I sure do. And not on some moldy old tombstone like the whites do. I want to go down in history as the greatest Shoshone fighter who ever lived."

"When this is over, remind me to have a talk with you."

"What about?"

Nate was spared from having to answer by the timely appearance of Winona, who entwined her fingers with his and indicated the orange ball hanging low in the western sky.

"It will not be long now, husband."

Two hours until nightfall, Nate reckoned. "Let the NunumBi come. We're as ready as we'll ever be."

"Are we really?"

The big mountain man said nothing. In almost two decades of marriage he'd never lied to her. He wasn't about to start now.

Chapter Nine

"I don't like this, Pa," Zachary King whispered. "I don't like it one bit."

"Hush. Any minute now the NunumBi will show up."

That was exactly what bothered Zach. The idea of his mother and the girls being alone in the cabin below had him worried sick. He should be with them. He should be there to protect Lou. Not up on the roof of the cabin. About to complain, he tensed when his father motioned for silence.

Nate had detected movement in the pines, furtive rustlings and the faint padding of small feet. Fireflies flared, only they weren't really fireflies, they were hellish red eyes. He counted ten, twelve, fourteen, sixteen, more than he had bargained for. The creatures glided swiftly from the northwest, fanning out as they drew near. His mouth went dry, his palms grew slick. The moment of truth had come.

Easing forward, Nate peered over the edge of the roof at the front of the cabin. No light spilled from within, not with the windows boarded up and the door shut. He prayed he had done the right thing, prayed his plan worked. If it didn't, the outcome would be too horrible to contemplate.

The hideous beings from the dawn of time were almost to the clearing. As if on cue, every one of them halted just shy of the high piles of brush spaced at regular intervals around the perimeter. Red orbs moved from side to side. The creatures were studying the situation, assessing whether the piles posed a threat. Presently they advanced, but slowly, warily.

To Zach, those disembodied eyes floating over the ground were so inhuman, so unnerving, he shivered and nervously ran a hand over the lid to the hot pot he held. It would be soon now. Very soon.

Nate saw the creatures stop again, this time at the belt of dry branches he'd laid down. A low trilling arose, mixed with guttural snarls and hisses. Were they trying to make sense of what he had done? Would they realize what he was up to? Or would they assume the branches were to give them away by the noise they'd create crossing?

Everything depended on what the little monsters did next. Nate's whole scheme hinged on it. A grim grin creased his lips when some of them bore to the right and the rest bore to the left to go around the barrier.

As quietly as stalking wolves, the NunumBi moved toward the door and windows, their goblin forms bent low, their claws glinting dully in the starlight. Their scarlet eyes were intent on the cabin. Not once did one of them think to check the roof. Not once did one of them glance up.

A common failing. Shakespeare McNair had taught Nate how to exploit it on the first hunt the two of them went on, many years ago. "Your best bet, Horatio, is to find a comfortable tree to roost in, near where elk and deer drink or graze, and wait for one to stroll by. Savvy as those critters are, they hardly ever look above them. Same with most everything else, including men, white or red. Three or four times I've saved my hide by hiding in trees when hostiles were after me."

The eight elfin shapes were now ranged along the front of the cabin, two at each window and four at the door. They were signaling back and forth, which Nate took as a prelude to an attack. One pressed an ear to the door, listening. Nate glanced at his son and nodded.

Zach lifted the pot's lid, then carefully set it aside. In the pot were glowing coals from the fireplace. Quickly, he added kindling from a parfleche crammed with grass and twigs. As soon as it caught and tiny flames blazed to life, Zach snatched up one of the torches beside him and lowered the end bound in cloth into the pot. When the cloth ignited, he passed the torch to his father and grabbed another.

Nate rose onto his knees, gauging the distance. He waited for the second torch to be lit and handed to him, then he hurled one after the other, the first at the belt of dry branches, the second at a pile of brush at the clearing's edge. Both hit their mark and flames erupted, spreading swiftly.

The creatures whirled. Those nearest the belt of branches flung arms across their faces to shield their eyes from the bright glare.

"You throw the rest!" Nate instructed. Jamming his Hawken to his shoulder, he leaned out and aimed at a NunumBi by the door. It was one of several that glanced upward. And like its fellows, it attempted to bolt.

Nate stroked the trigger smoothly. The boom of the smoothbore slammed the hairy dwarf to the earth, where it lay convulsing, its tapered teeth bared. The rest were fleeing, screening their sensitive eyes as they rushed toward either end of the clearing. Nate dropped a hand to a pistol.

Zach had lit a third torch. Rising, he threw it at a pile of brush off to the right. His part in his father's plan called for him to set as many piles alight as he could, thereby blinding the NunumBi and keeping them pinned close to the cabin so his father could pick them off. The torch flew true, and in the blaze of fire and light that ensued, Zach saw one of the creatures turn toward him and raise a small object.

Nate saw it, too. He snapped off a shot, but he was a shade too slow. There was an audible twang.

Searing pain lanced Zach's shoulder. He looked down at a tiny feathered shaft jutting from the buckskin, so puny as to make him chuckle. "I'm hit, Pa," he said, "but not bad." Hardly had he spoken when a terrible burning sensation spread down his arm and chest with frightening speed. He broke out in a sweat and felt his pulse increase.

"Son?" Nate said.

Zach tried to answer, but his tongue had become as thick as a cow's. The burning sensation was seeping into his legs, into his hands and fingers, and he could barely move. He tried to tell his pa, but his lips were numb. His face prickled as from a heat rash, his neck was wooden, and he had to fight to swallow.

"Zachary?" Nate repeated, forgetting the NunumBi. His son's features were pasty and slick. Nate sprang to him. "Say something!"

Zach wanted to, but he was almost totally paralyzed. His arms, his legs, couldn't move. A whine escaped him as his knees buckled and he pitched forward. Fortunately for him, his father was there to catch him and gently lower him to the roof.

"What's wrong?" Nate asked anxiously. Spying the arrow, he gripped it and wrenched it out. On the tip was a tiny sawtooth barb of a sickly sulfurous hue. He sniffed it and jerked back at the foul odor. "Dear God. No!" The barb had been dipped in poison, a common practice among some Indian tribes. Usually rattlesnake venom was used. Or arrowheads were dipped in the kidneys of dead skunks or other animals. One whiff was enough for a mountaineer to determine which type of toxin was involved, but in this case Nate couldn't.

Zach struggled to lift a hand and failed. His arms, his upper chest, his face were turning as wooden as his neck. He had no feeling in them at all. *I'm dying*! he thought, and wanted to screech in outrage, but his vocal cords had seized up. Another few moments and he would be gone.

Inside the cabin, Winona King was braced for an onslaught, a pistol in either hand. She didn't like being cooped up, didn't like being bait. But with the door barred and boards over the windows, she and the girls were safe enough. Evelyn and Lou were by the table, each with a pistol, each craning her neck as Winona was doing, to hear what was going on outside.

Winona had heard muffled sounds on the roof, then two shots. Grizzly Killer and Stalking Coyote had sprung the trap! Her natural inclination was to throw the door open and assist them, but her husband was depending on her to safeguard the girls. She must stay put. It was up to her to keep the creatures from breaking in.

Each passing moment was an eternity. Winona strained to hear more shots, to have some clue as to how her mate and her son were faring. But there were none. No shouts. No screams. Nothing. The suspense mounted until it was unbearable.

"Ma, what's going on out there?" Evelyn asked.

Winona had to find out. "Both of you stay right where you are. I will see." She lunged for the door, stopping when a loud thud sounded.

"It's those things!" Evelyn cried.

The pounding continued. Aiming low, Winona was ready to shoot when her name was hollered.

"It's me, Nate! Open up! Hurry!"

The urgency in her husband's voice alarmed Winona. It had an edge to it, a hint of raw desperation not typical of him. Removing the bar, she learned why.

Nate was carrying Zach, clutching his son to his chest. He'd had to sling Zach over a shoulder when he clambered down from the roof, nearly losing his grip in the grooves he'd gouged in the logs. Zach was motionless, stiff, and cold. "The NunumBi shot him with an arrow," Nate disclosed as he hustled to their bed. "The tip was poisoned."

"Zach!" The scream wasn't torn from Winona or Lou. It was Evelyn who flung herself at her brother and tried to throw her arms around him in a fit of woe.

Nate pulled his daughter aside so his wife could examine their son. Winona was the healer in the family, her knowledge of herbs

David Thompson

and cures extensive. She knew how to treat everything from warts to croup. Poison, though, wasn't an illness. "Can you do anything for him?"

Winona ran her fingers over Zach's face and neck. She probed for a vein to take his pulse, which was so weak it was a wonder he was still alive. His vitals were affected, his bodily functions slowed and close to stopping. Although his eyes were wide open and clear, no hint of life animated them.

"Can you?" Nate pressed her.

"I don't know what kind of poison they used," Winona said. Even knowing might not help. Some were so fast-acting, remedies were useless. "I fear we are losing him."

Louisa was at the foot of the bed, riveted by shock so intense, she was as paralyzed as her betrothed. *She couldn't lose him!* Not before they were married! Not before they had lived many long and happy years together! His face was chalky, his chest as still as the breath she was holding. Her fingers, grasping the quilt, were clenched so tight they hurt.

Nate opened his ammo pouch and took out the small arrow, holding it by the feathers. "This is what they used."

Winona sniffed the barbed tip as he had done and reacted in the same fashion. "The legends of my people claim the NunumBi dipped their arrows in the blood of giant winged lizards. There is no known cure."

Refusing to accept their son was a goner, Nate snapped, "There must be something we can do! Try those roots you use for rattlesnake bites."

Evelyn, sniffling loudly, tugged at her father's britches. "Pa?"

"Not now, little one," Nate said. He placed a hand on his son's brow and was filled with consternation at how icy Zach had become. Touching him was like touching one of the glaciers high up in the mountains.

"But Pa!" Evelyn tugged again.

"What is it?" Nate asked testily. She should know better than to interfere at so critical a moment.

"Is the cabin going to catch on fire?" Evelyn pointed.

Nate had forgotten about the belt of branches and the piles of brush. A high sheet of flame formed a blistering barrier between the cabin and the forest, lighting up the clearing as if it were the middle of the day. He ran to the doorway and saw that none of the fires had spread to neighboring trees. The woods and their cabin were safe.

None of the NunumBi were anywhere in sight. Nate figured the bright light had driven them off, and since the fires wouldn't die out for a while, he had no qualms about shutting the door partway and shutting the creatures from his mind. "What can we do for Zach?" was all he cared about.

In a parfleche suspended from a peg were most of the leaves, stems, and roots Winona relied on to prepare her medicines. Her supply had to be constantly replenished, a tedious but essential task if her potions and ointments were to be effective. Upending the parfleche on the counter, she sorted through elderberry roots—or duhiembuh, as her people called them—which were used to reduce inflammation; the raw leaves of plantain, which were applied to battle wounds; yarrow, or pannonzia, for toothache; and, at last, the one she was after, the rare root of a certain cactus plant.

Taking one of the many pots already filled with water, Winona put it on the tripod over the fire. "We must make some tea."

"What does that root do?" Nate asked. She had so many cures, he couldn't keep track of them.

"It—how do you say . . . ?" In her agitated state, Winona couldn't think of the right word. "It stimulates the heart and the blood."

Nate noticed Louisa, tears streaming down her cheeks, her knuckles white as a bedsheet. She needed something to do, something to take her thoughts off Zach. "I could use some coffee," he lied. "To keep me awake the rest of the night in case the NunumBi come back." When she didn't so much as blink, he nudged her. "Did you hear me, Louisa?"

"What? What was that?" Lou had heard him, yes, but as if from a great distance. "Sorry, Mr. King," she blurted. "Coffee,

121

you said? Give me ten minutes and I'll have a batch brewed.''

"Take your time," Nate responded. Squeezing his son's limp hand, he moved back to the door. "I won't be a minute. I left our rifles up on the roof."

Winona was slicing the root into thin strips and dropping them in the water. "No, husband!" she virtually shouted. "Do not go out alone! Wait until the tea is done and Lou or I will go with you."

"If that's what you want," Nate said to spare her added anxiety. The Hawkens would be safe enough. In the meantime, he could use hers or his daughter's if the creatures reappeared. Which wasn't likely.

Nate involuntarily jumped when small hands encircled his right leg, reminding him that he was neglecting someone. "How are you holding up, princess?"

Evelyn's eyes were moist, her nose running. "I'm fine, Pa," she said so softly he could barely hear. "But I'm awful worried about Zach. He's as cold as one of those icicles that hang from the cabin in the winter."

Nate tried to make her smile. "Weren't you the one who said she'd be happy if the Blackfeet would kidnap him and never give him back?"

"I never really meant that, Pa," Evelyn said, and burst out bawling. She had said a lot of mean things to her brother, things she now wished she hadn't, things she would never say again if only he would live!

Seldom did Evelyn cry. When she did, Winona was always on hand to comfort her, and now Nate looked to his wife to do so again. But Winona was busy with the tea. It was up to him. "There, there," he said for lack of anything better, and patted her heaving shoulders. "Your brother is as ornery as you are. He'll pull through."

Evelyn bawled harder, her face buried against his leggings.

Nate was at a loss what else to do, so he hugged her and let her cry herself out. Tears were foreign to him. In the King household in New York it had been forbidden for him or his brothers to "indulge in unmanly behavior," or they suffered his father's wrath. He'd never had a sister. And his mother, if she shed tears now and again, did so in private.

Now, gazing at his son, Nate felt an urge to shed some tears of his own, but he held them in. It wasn't that he thought he had an example to set, as his father always had. Or that he branded it wrong for a man to weep. No, he didn't want to cry, because he feared that once he started, he couldn't stop.

"Please recover, son," Nate said, profoundly sorry that Zach couldn't see or hear him.

Unknown to the mountain man or anyone else, the exact opposite was true. Zachary King was fully aware of everything going on around him. His eyes and ears worked just fine, but he had no means of letting everyone else know. His body was as rigid as a board, his fingers as stiff as iron. He couldn't open his mouth any wider than it was; he couldn't utter a sound, not a single, solitary syllable. Yet his mind was active, his thoughts as clear as the lake. Whatever had been on the tip of that arrow affected only his body.

It tore Zach apart to see his fiancée in turmoil. When Lou had been staring at him in heartsick love, her eyes glistening, he'd tried to twitch, to speak. But it was hopeless. His conscious self was trapped in a living log.

Zach was thankful in one regard: He was still alive. Whatever the NunumBi used had just rendered him helpless. Maybe it was how the NunumBi took captives.

Into view stepped his mother, who sat beside him and tenderly ran a hand across his cheek. Zach couldn't feel her finger, but he could see how sad she was. He longed to be able to say something, to ease her sorrow.

"It will not be long, Stalking Coyote. The tea should help you."

Zach attempted to move his eyeballs. Just a smidgen, just enough to show her he could. He might as well have tried to move a mountain.

David Thompson

"Do not die on us, son, please," Winona said, leaning down and kissing his cheek. Her eyes were shiny wet, her voice raspy. "I have probably not said it as often as I should, but I love you. You make me proud to be your mother. One day you will be a great Shoshone warrior, with a lovely wife and a fine lodge and more horses than you can count on your fingers and toes." She mustered a grin.

Were Zach able to, he would have given her a squeeze that would break her ribs.

Winona spoke in a whisper. "You *must* live, my son. For my sake if not your own. That might sound selfish, but no parent should ever lose a child. We lose a part of our heart, and we are never the same afterward."

Zach thought his eyes might mist over, but evidently he couldn't cry, either.

"At moments like this I always remember when you were little," Winona went on. "Cute as a prairie dog, you were. I remember how you tottered when you took your first steps. How loud you howled that time the chipmunk bit your finger."

The mangy chipmunk had been eating out of his hand, Zach recollected. The ungrateful varmint.

"I'll never forget the day your father gave you a pony and you hopped around like a jackrabbit, giggling and clapping. Or the day you made your first kill, a squirrel, and were so proud of yourself. You were ready to slay a bear next." Winona chuckled. "You have brought us so much happiness."

Zach could only stare blankly upward as she kissed his chin, stood, and walked toward the fireplace. No one else was close enough for him to see, but he heard Evelyn crying and a pot clang. He assumed she was upset because of the attack. It certainly couldn't be on his account.

Zach would very much have liked to close his eyes and rest, but his mind was racing like the wind and his eyelids wouldn't move. Chafing at his inability to do anything, he brightened when the girl who had won his heart took his mother's place beside him. She held a coffeepot, which she lowered to her lap as she bent low.

"Oh, my darling. I am so scared I will lose you."

Her beautiful eyes mirrored sadness as deep as Winona's. Concentrating with all his might, Zach sought to move his lips but couldn't.

Lou glanced up as if to make sure no one else was near them. Then her mouth brushed his. "I never thought I could love anyone like I love you, Zachary King. I always took it for granted I would never marry. That other girls might fall in love and live happily ever after, but not me." She paused. "After my dad was killed, I hated all Indians. Hated everything to do with them. I thought it would be best if every filthy savage was wiped off the face of the earth."

This was news to Zach, and he did not quite know how to take it.

"I changed when you came into my life. I realized I couldn't hate all Indians because of what a few had done. There are good Indians and bad ones, just as there are God-fearing whites and cutthroats who would slit a person from ear to ear for the thrill of it."

Zach was still mulling over that "filthy savage" business.

"Somehow you touched my soul, Zach King. You reached deep inside of me and made me whole again. You filled me with love instead of hate. And for that, and a million other reasons, I will love you as long as I live."

Zach knew she was kissing his neck and ear, but he couldn't feel the kisses, he could only hear the light smack of her lips. When she straightened, she was crying.

"Don't die on me, darn you. I'm looking forward to being your wife. To having a cabin of our own and a passel of little ones underfoot. To the kind of life I've always dreamed about, the kind I wished I'd had growing up. So live. Please."

As much as Zach would have liked to oblige her, it wasn't entirely up to him. It depended on the substance the arrow had injected into his system and whether it would wear off or make him worse than he already was.

"I'll come sit with you after I fix your pa some coffee." Lou blew him a kiss and moved off the bed.

Zach had a lot to think about, but he was denied the opportunity. Much to his amazement, his little sister now plopped herself where Lou had been, and sniffled.

"I'm sorry for all the hurtful things I ever said to you, Stalking Coyote."

Zach wondered if his hearing was starting to go.

"I'm sorry for all the squabbles we've had, for always giving you a hard time, for not treating you nicer."

Either his ears were going or Zach was hallucinating. This couldn't be his sister talking. The poison was seeping into his brain. Pretty soon she would hug him and say she loved him, proof he wasn't long for the world.

"Oh, my poor brother!" Evelyn mewed, and flung her arms across his chest. "Please don't die. I love you too much, and want you to go on being my brother for a long time to come!"

There it was, Zach reflected. Any second now he would start seeing those pink buffalo of Otter Tail's. The NunumBi were evil incarnate to kill a man this way. Strip him of control of his body, then strip him of his reasoning, of his mind. A slow, awful death, made immeasurably worse by the feeling of helplessness.

Evelyn was weeping and whimpering. "Please, please, please."

Zach saw her hand rise to his cheek. He couldn't deny the obvious any longer. She really was upset. She really was worried. She really did care.

Sniffling and wiping her nose with a sleeve, Evelyn sat up. "There's so much I'd like to tell you. Remember that time your wolf cub chewed your moccasins? Well, he did it because I smeared bear fat on them. I was mad at you for teasing me." She coughed. "And that time you couldn't find your fish hooks and they turned up at the bottom of Ma's sewing kit? I put them there after you called me names."

The little imp! Zach recalled half a dozen other incidents he would like to ask her about.

"I know I've been a thorn in your side at times. I'm sorry. Truly sorry. It's not that I hate you or anything. It's just how brothers and sisters are, I reckon."

Zach didn't hate her, either. From what his friends said about their sisters, she wasn't all that bad compared to some.

Evelyn suddenly stiffened and shifted around, dabbing at her eyes. "Pa? Where are you going? Ma wanted you to wait."

His father didn't respond. Zach tried to twist his neck to see the door, but it was a waste of effort. Intensely curious to know what was happening, he was given some idea when his sister threw back her head and screamed.

Chapter Ten

Nate King had been standing in the doorway watching smoke billow skyward when he noticed what he mistook for a tree limb near the door, at the base of the cabin. Then he looked down. It was a foot, a small, hair-covered foot, and it was twitching.

Belatedly, Nate remembered the creature he had shot from up on the roof. He hadn't seen it fall, hadn't any idea he'd hit it. Zach's plight had commanded all his attention. Now Nate drew a pistol and leaped into the open, a wave of heat roasting him as he squatted and thrust the muzzle at the figure sprawled against the wall.

The garish, dancing firelight highlighted the creature's hellish countenance. It was limp—but was it dead? A dark pool had formed, blood from a bullet hole high on its sloping forehead. Blood as thick as pea soup and about the same color.

Nate poked it with the flintlock, but there was no reaction. Not taking anything for granted, he prodded it several more times. The foot didn't stop twitching, but that could just as well have been a death spasm as a sign of life. Gingerly, as if he were reaching for a rattlesnake, Nate poked a shoulder with his finger. It was like poking a slab of rock.

Nate gripped its left wrist and pulled it farther into the light. The NunumBi was much heavier than its slight stature would have led him to believe, its compact sinews as dense as marble. He placed his hand flat against its chest but felt no heartbeat. Which might not mean much, since the creatures might not possess the same internal organs as humans.

Grunting, Nate lifted it off the ground. He estimated its weight at somewhere between eighty and ninety pounds. Holding it at arm's length, he entered the cabin. Evelyn saw him and screeched like a banshee.

Winona was stirring the tea, Lou next to her, waiting to put the coffeepot on. They both gasped, and Lou swayed as if she might faint.

Resisting a gushing tide of panic, Winona moved to the bed to comfort her trembling daughter. "Husband, is that thing dead? Is it safe to bring it in here?"

Based on the bullet hole, Nate had to say yes. The ball had entered above the creatures bushy brows and exited where the skull connected to the neck, coring its brain. Greenish ooze matted the short hairs on its shoulders and had trickled under its left arm and down its side. The beast had an odor not unlike that of a ferret or mink. Either it had scent glands or it never bathed.

Nate deposited his burden on the table, flat on its back, and spread out the arms and legs. The slanted eyes, the feral nose, the sharp teeth and chin, the pointed ears—the NunumBi was a bestial aberration, a deviate, a violation of the natural order.

Ironically, when Nate had first heard about them, he'd pictured the NunumBi as hairy Fair Folk, akin to the Little People of England and Europe, the exotic pixies and delightful fairies of myth and literature. But the reality couldn't have been further from the truth. NunumBi weren't light, airy, ethereal beings. They were dark and ugly and wicked, a blight on all that was and ever had been or would be, beings of nightmare and madness. They should not exist, yet they did. It made a man question every fundamental value he held dear.

Evelyn had stopped screaming, but she was clinging to her mother and quaking like an aspen leaf. She couldn't help herself. The creatures filled her to overflowing with potent fear such as she had never known. "I don't want that thing in our cabin, Ma! I don't!"

Nor did Winona, but her intense curiosity would not be denied. Until the previous night, no Shoshone had seen a NunumBi for more winters than anyone in her tribe could remember. No one had examined a dead one since the dawn of time, when the great war was waged and the creatures were driven into hiding. So holding Evelyn close, she slowly approached the table, half afraid the fiend would leap up and pounce on them.

On the bed, Zach King was mad enough to cuss an unending streak. He gathered that his pa had brought one of the hairy devils inside. He'd give anything to see it, and pound the little brute to a pulp for what they had done to him.

Nate had set his pistol down to give the thing a thorough going-over. Its short hairs were hard and stiff, almost like quills, which explained why arrows were prone to glance off. The skin, too, was hard, much tougher than human skin, yet incredibly pliant, like putty. The claws weren't quite razor sharp, but they could disembowel an adversary as handily as a sword.

Its teeth were even more formidable. In effect, the mouth bristled with miniature knives, more than a panther or wolverine could boast. They were the teeth of a meat eater, or, to be more precise, of a predator. Which brought up this question: What did the NunumBi eat?

The head was obscenely big for so runtish a body. As Nate examined its neck, he discovered a thin strap attached to a small pouch that nestled snug under the NunumBi's right arm. Prying the drawstring open, Nate found four of the tiny arrows that had felled his son along with a small bow and a thimble-size container made of clear crystal. "Will you look at these!" he marveled.

The bow was made of bone, a single curved bone unlike any

Nate was familiar with. It did not come from any animal he'd ever carved up, which included practically every species in the Rockies. The string was sinew but not buffalo sinew, as the Shoshones favored. It resembled those found in panthers.

All the arrows had been crafted from wood, though not ash or oak or pine or any wood Nate could identify. The feathers were unique in themselves, each a striking blue. A deep, dark blue, not the lighter shade of a jay or bluebird.

The upshot was that all the creature's possessions were as alien as the NunumBi. Wherever it called home, there also dwelled birds and beasts not found anywhere else.

Next Nate puzzled over the small container. The crystal was as smooth as glass and had sparkling facets, like a diamond. By experimenting, he learned the top could be twisted off, revealing a gooey orange substance that stank to high heaven, the same substance the dwarfs tipped their arrows with. "Here's the stuff that laid Zach low," he said, giving the container to his wife. "Do you have any idea what it is?"

Winona had none whatsoever. It wasn't plant residue. Nor did she think it was venom. Perhaps, she concluded, the creatures mixed it from special ingredients. Her best hope was still the root medicine, which sent her hurrying to the pot to check whether the water was boiling.

Nate put everything back in the pouch and set it on the counter. As for the creature, he would bury it in the morning. In the meantime, he covered it with a blanket so it wouldn't frighten the girls any more than was necessary.

Winona was filling a cup with simmering tea. "We would all be happier if you took the NunumBi outside. I do not want it in my lodge overnight."

Every husband, early in every marriage, becomes aware there are instances when it is acceptable to stand up to his wife and instances when it is not. Nate rated this one of the latter. Offering no protest, he wrapped the blanket around the dwarf and lugged it out, setting it down exactly where he had found it.

"Thank you, husband," Winona called out, extremely grateful. The thing's mere presence had spooked her.

Nate scanned the clearing. Most of the branches had been charred to embers and would soon burn out. He considered lighting more brush piles but opted to save them for when they were really needed. Closing the door behind him, he asked, "How soon before we can fetch those rifles?" Every gun was crucial to their survival, and he wouldn't put it past the NunumBi to climb up on the roof and steal them.

Winona had just sat on the edge of the bed. "We can do it now if you like. Louisa will tend Stalking Coyote."

Lou was placing the coffeepot over the fire. "No, you go right ahead, Mrs. King," she said. "I'll help your husband. We won't be but a minute." She couldn't bear to look at Zach. It tore her apart.

"I'll go with you too, Pa," Evelyn said.

Nate palmed both of his pistols. "Stay with your mother, little one, in case she needs anything."

Evelyn was no fool. She saw right through him. But she nodded, secretly glad she need not brave the darkness and the demons who dwelled in it.

Nate waited for Lou to join him, gave her a reassuring smile, and opened the door. By now the belt of branches had almost burned itself out, but the piles of brush cast enough light to reveal no NunumBi were in the vicinity. Sliding out, he crept to the left and was almost to the corner when she whispered his name.

Lou was pointing at the base of the wall. "Isn't this where you put that awful thing?" She had been worried she might step on it and had made a point to look for the bundled blanket.

The dead one was gone! Nate crouched, pulling her down with him, and braced for an assault that didn't materialize. "Go back in the cabin," he whispered. "I'll get the rifles."

"What? Why?" Lou would do no such thing. "I said I'd help you, and I will. Don't fret on my account. I can shoot as straight as the next fellow." She hefted her flintlock, hiding the stark fear that threatened to turn her legs to mush.

David Thompson

Against Nate's better judgment, he went on. Knowing the NunumBi might be out there, watching, made every yard they covered fraught with menace. Rounding the corner, he stalked to where the grooves had been carved in the logs. "You go up first. I'll follow." He didn't want the girl out of his sight.

"Why both of us?" Lou responded. "We can get this over with faster if I stay here and stand guard."

She was right, but Nate hesitated. A couple of rifles weren't worth her life. His son was already at death's door; he'd be damned if he would lose her too.

"Go, Mr. King," Lou insisted, touching his arm. "I'll be fine. Really."

Scowling, Nate faced the cabin, stuck both pistols under his belt, and started up. Twice he paused to scour the woods. At the top, he twisted. "If you hear or see anything, give a holler."

"They'll hear me in St. Louis," Lou quipped, her teeth flashing white. She was putting on a brave front for his benefit.

Nate hurried. The rifles were right where they had been left, along with the parfleche crammed with kindling and the pot containing the coals. Bundling everything in his arms, he retraced his steps and leaned down. "Here. I'll hand you the Hawkens and—"

Lou wasn't there.

A low cry came from under the trees. Short figures were swarming over a taller one, who resisted valiantly. Red eyes swirled like tiny shooting stars.

Nate launched himself from the roof. He bent his knees to absorb the shock, but he still landed hard and stumbled, almost falling on his face. By the time he righted himself and set down everything except for one rifle, the combatants had moved deeper into the forest. One or two of the creatures appeared to be clinging to Lou's shoulders; others had steely arms looped around her lower legs.

"Mr. King! Help me!" she managed to cry before one of the NunumBi clamped a hand over her mouth, stifling her shouts.

Lord help him, Nate tried. He sprinted in pursuit, shrieking a war cry, and a dozen scarlet eyes were fixed on him. Firing into their midst might bring one down, but the ball might also strike Lou, so he didn't shoot. Nate pushed himself to overtake them, but soon the red eyes were mere pinpoints. Lou's figure was lost amid the many tree trunks. The NunumBi and their captive were moving away from him with incredible rapidity.

Nate ran another twenty yards. Then he stopped in baffled outrage. They were gone! The NunumBi were bearing Louisa to their lair, and there wasn't a damn thing he could do to stop them!

Raising his fists to the heavens, Nate roared. She had been snatched from under his very nose! But the creatures had made no attempt to harm him. Why? Did they want to humiliate him? To show he was powerless against them?

Nate tried to think as he imagined they would. Had they abducted Lou in retribution for the death of one of their own? Was taking her their way of making him suffer for his affront? To what end, though? What would they do with her? The most obvious answer, the reason Apaches and Blackfeet stole white women, didn't apply. Would they make a slave of her? Torture and then slay her?

For some reason the image of the dead NunumBi's mouth floated before Nate, and he had a horrific premonition. Those rapier teeth. So sharp. Designed to rip and shred flesh. *Human* flesh, possibly?

Nate ran to the cabin, snatched the other rifle, and sped to the front. The door was open, his wife just inside with her own Hawken.

Winona took one look at him and blanched. "No!" She'd heard yells and her husband's bellow and had known something was wrong, but she couldn't leave her son and daughter alone to investigate.

"Lou's not dead, but she may soon be," Nate confirmed. "They grabbed her, and there was nothing I could do." Shame bent his head as he followed her in, barred the door, and sagged against it. He could never forgive himself. It was his fault, plain and simple. He'd lost his son's fiancée and maybe his son, all because he'd given his word they could stay to help him fight the NunumBi. *All because of his stupid word.* Thank goodness Zach was oblivious to what was going on, Nate mused. The shock of Lou's abduction might be all it took to finish what the poison had started.

Zach King, however, had heard every word. Raw panic surged through him, and he tried with all his might to rise but couldn't. His body still refused to obey his mental commands. It was just like all the other times, with one small difference. The tips of his fingers and toes began to tingle.

To his dying day Zach never knew with certainty what broke the toxin's hold. Was it hearing of his beloved's capture? Was it the tea his mother had forced down his throat? Had the effects of whatever was on the tip of the arrow started to wear off? Or was it a combination of all three?

The tingling spread up his limbs, to his knees and elbows. It hurt—hurt like the dickens—but Zach welcomed the pain. It was proof that feeling was being restored to his body, that soon he might be able to move.

Again and again Zach tried. He willed his fingers to bend, his toes to curl. Neither would, but he didn't give up. He focused on the little finger on his right hand and kept commanding it to *move, move, move.* The tingling grew worse, much worse, to the point where, had he been able, he'd have screamed. Then the miracle occurred. He felt his little finger bend ever so slightly, not more than a fraction of a inch. It encouraged him to persevere, to keep at it.

Zach saw his mother walk by, a study in misery. She glanced at him, and he moved his finger again, but in her state she didn't notice.

"What will you do, Pa?" he heard Evelyn ask.

"Go after her in the morning."

"Alone?" This from Zach's mother.

"It can't be helped. You have to stay and watch over them. If I'm not back by late afternoon, saddle your horses and light a shuck for Shakespeare's. Go west to the pass so you can stay shy of the NunumBi.''

Zach could move two fingers! The wooden sensation was fading, but not fast enough to suit him.

"No argument, Winona," his father said. "I've got to do what I can. I could never live with myself if I didn't.''

"What about Zach, Pa?" Evelyn said. She had always been a bundle of questions. "How will we take him with us?"

"Rig a travois.''

Zach would spare himself the indignity. Shoshones and other tribes transported lodges and personal effects on a framework of long poles. They also used the travois to carry the aged and infirm, or pregnant women too heavy with child to walk or ride. No self-respecting warrior would ever let himself be tied to one.

"It is a long, hard climb to the pass," his mother remarked. "And it is very cold that high up at night.''

"You're quibbling," Nate said. "Bundle him in his bearskin robe and he'll be fine. Go slow on those switchbacks when you descend. And when you reach Shakespeare's, don't let him come here alone.''

"I wish there were another way, husband.''

"That makes two of us, wife.''

There *was* another way, as Zach would show them. He could partly flex his right hand and wriggle his left foot, and he was working furiously on the others. Every part of him tingled now, toe to head, though the tingling was fading in his extremities even as it increased in his chest and neck. Zach's right hand closed all the way, his fingertips brushing his palm. Pleased, he nearly smiled, forgetting he couldn't, and the corner of his mouth quirked upward a bit. His tongue rubbed the roof of his mouth.

Zach fought to make a sound, any sound, to get his family's attention. A tiny whine escaped his lips, but no one heard. He experimented, shifting his eyes to see where everyone was, and his eyeballs moved just as they should have. His ma was by the fireplace, his pa by the door, both about as wretchedly forlorn as two people could be. Evelyn was at the table, her cheeks streaked with dry tears, her chin in her hands.

Look at me! Zach yearned to shout. Another whine had to suffice. His vocal cords were loosening up, but at a snail's pace. He lifted his right hand an inch off the bed and wriggled his fingers, thinking to catch his sister's attention. In vain. She was interested only in moping, at which she was an expert. The last time she'd been in the doldrums, she'd sulked around the cabin for a week.

Zach slid his tongue to the front of his mouth, against his upper teeth. He thought he could whistle, but only puffed feebly.

His mother walked toward his father. She had to pass the bed again, and as she did, Zach exerted every ounce of energy he had. A teeny noise, like the *cheep* of a baby chick, was the best he could do. It was enough to make *him* want to cry.

Winona was lost in thought, plotting how she could refuse to do as her husband wanted without angering him. She positively refused to leave him. He could rant, he could rave, but unless he trussed her up and threw her over a horse, she was staying at his side, as a wife should.

Still, Winona told herself, it would help to have a reason he would accept. A logical reason, since men were swayed more by their heads than their hearts. She was going by the bed when a peculiar chirp, like the peep of a bird, intruded on her plotting. Her son was staring at her with the strangest expression, his mouth puckered as if he had tasted bitter food. Winona took another step, then the significance slammed her around and she gripped him by the shoulders, squealing, "Stalking Coyote is recovering! Grizzly Killer! Blue Flower! Come quick!"

They did, the air of melancholy replaced by glee. Evelyn clambered onto the quilt and wormed around to her brother's other side. "His eyes moved, Ma! I saw them! And look at how funny his mouth is!"

Zach didn't find anything humorous about it. His body was bending to his will, but some of his muscles were going through brief contortions, an aftereffect, apparently, of the paralysis.

Nate gripped his son's hand and felt Zach match the pressure. "He's trying to say something."

"What do you reckon it is?" Evelyn asked.

They would soon learn, Zach thought. His tongue was moving freely, but his vocal cords weren't quite restored to normal. He grunted. He growled. He gurgled. His father, mother, and sister all leaned toward him, eager to hear his first words. But there was only one that needed to be said. He concentrated, strained, parted his lips, and hummed like an oversized bee. Finally, he ended their suspense by blurting, *"No!"*

Winona, Nate, and Evelyn looked at one another.

"No what?" Evelyn said.

"No, he isn't recovering?" Nate speculated.

"No, he doesn't want more tea?" was Winona's guess.

Zach sucked in a breath and got the rest out in a rush. "No, none of us are going anywhere! Except after Lou! She's part of our family now. She's going to be my wife. So as soon as I can stand, we're leaving. We won't abandon her. Do you hear me, Pa? Do you hear me, Ma? You wouldn't turn your backs on Evelyn or me, and we're not turning our backs on her!"

Evelyn was flabbergasted. Her brother had never talked to their parents so harshly before, and she tensed for the tongue-lashing he was sure to receive. Unbelievably, neither her father nor her mother was mad. They smiled at him, then at each other. "Aren't you going to punish him?" Evelyn asked.

"What for?" Nate said, and clapped his son on the back. "A man has the right to speak his mind."

"But when I do that, you call it giving you sass," Evelyn pointed out. "And since when is he a man?"

Winona shushed her. "It is not very kind of you to tease him at a time like this. I am very disappointed in you, Blue Flower."

Zach raised and lowered his arms. He pumped his legs back and forth, the quilt jouncing on his knees. Another five minutes and he would be well enough to get up. "Better go saddle the horses, Pa. It won't be long now."

Nate stayed where he was. "I said you had the right to speak your mind. I didn't say I agreed to do as you wanted. You and I will head out tomorrow at first light.''

"And leave Lou at the mercy of those things all night?'' Zach would never agree, not in a million years.

"We can't track them in the dark, son. They know that. Maybe taking Louisa was a ruse to lure us all outside so they can jump us.'' Nate felt it wise not to mention the other possibility, their need for fresh meat. "We need rest, and plenty of it, to hold our own against the NunumBi. I'll take first watch, your mother will take the second, you can have the third. An hour before sunrise, wake us up. It's the best we can do under the circumstances.''

Zach heartily disagreed, but he didn't say so. Pretending to give in, he slumped against the headboard. "I reckon you know better than me how we should go about this. We'll do it your way.''

"I'm glad you agree,'' Nate said, impressed by his son's maturity.

"I'd like to take first watch, though, if you don't mind,'' Zach said, hastily explaining out of dread that his father would refuse. "I'm too wide awake to sleep, Pa. It's that stuff they shot into me. It has me jumpier than a frog in a frying pan.''

"It's fine by me.''

Plans were made. Nate had a few special items he wanted to take. They debated whether to use horses since the animals were skittish around the NunumBi. In due course, husband and wife turned in. Their daughter asked to sleep with them, saying her own blankets needed a washing. The fire burned low.

Zach King sat in the rocking chair, waiting impatiently. As soon as his parents and sister were asleep, he armed himself, silently opened the door, and slipped from the cabin. The love of his life needed him, and *nothing* was going to keep him from her.

Chapter Eleven

Louisa May Clark had never been so afraid in all her born days. She felt the fear in every fiber of her being, knifing outward from her core. And yet, the strange thing was, as scared as Lou felt, she didn't give in to it. She didn't scream or faint; she wasn't seized by paralysis and so weak she couldn't lift a finger to defend herself.

The opposite took place. Lou's fear lent her strength, lent her the will to fight back. Just as wood fueled a fire, fear fueled all her desire to go on living. She resisted the NunumBi with all she had, fighting like a tigress or a painter protecting her young.

Their initial rush had caught her flat-footed. Lou had glanced up at the roof, anxious for Nate King to reappear. She hadn't heard any sounds, she hadn't had the slightest notion the creatures were anywhere near until she looked around and there they were, almost on top of her with their hands stretching out to seize her.

Lou tried to shout. But the things piled on, over a dozen, some stripping her of weapons, some grabbing her legs, others her arms, while one bounded high onto her chest and clamped a furry palm over her mouth. Then they hauled her into the trees.

David Thompson

The creatures holding her legs started to lift her off the ground. By suddenly shifting her weight, Lou threw them off balance. She yanked her legs free, straightened, and started thrashing and bucking like a horse under the influence of loco weed. A NunumBi holding her arms scrambled lower and tried to get a grip on her ankles, but a foot to the face sent him sprawling. Jerking her left arm loose, she punched and battered those still clinging to her.

Lou experienced a glimmer of hope when Zach's pa ran to her rescue. She was tiring, though, which allowed the things to swarm over her again. They quickly bore her away from Nate and the cabin. Her future father-in-law valiantly sought to overtake them, but it was like a turtle trying to overtake an antelope. It just couldn't be done.

Lou's attempts to throw the NunumBi off became weaker, less frequent. She conserved her energy for when she would really need it, for when the creatures decided to dispose of her. As they surely would, for she was under no illusions about her impending fate. She was going to die. Very well, when the moment came, Lou would strive her utmost to hurt or slay as many of the creatures as she could. She would not die like a lamb led to slaughter. She would not die meekly.

Lou liked to think that her pa, gazing down from the hereafter, would be proud of her. That Zach would be proud of her.

Zach. Dwelling on him soothed her, calmed her, erasing most if not all of her fright. Lou keenly regretted they would never be man and wife. She'd looked forward to that so much. So very, very much. To be denied supreme happiness was tragic. She would have liked to hug him one last time, to kiss him, to whisper special endearments reserved for his ears and his alone.

The scrape of a claw across an arm brought Lou's reverie to an end. She had lost all sense of direction, but a glimpse of the constellations through a gap in the forest canopy showed the creatures were bearing her to the northeast. Six or seven were holding her, with as little effort as she would hold one of Evelyn's dolls.

Red eyes floated below her, to the right and to the left. When she stared at any of them, they stared back. Or, rather, glared back, for the blazing redness of their eyes matched the searing hatred they seemed to have for all humans. She wondered if the NunumBi hated people so much because of the great war waged long ago, or whether the hatred was itself the cause of the war. Maybe it was impossible for the dwarfs and humanity to exist in peace and friendship. Maybe the mutual loathing both had for each other was as old as the two races. Maybe it was part of their nature.

The creatures began talking in their guttural language, grunts, hisses, and trilling so alien as to make Lou want to cram her fingers in her ears to keep from hearing it.

Her abductors unexpectedly halted.

Lou could see trees and a nearby knoll. Several of the NunumBi squatted and roved their hands over the ground. To Lou, it looked as if they started to peel the top layer of sod back. A dank, earthy scent wafted to her nose as she was borne to the edge of a gaping cleft and the creatures started down.

Lou remembered the Shoshone legends, how the NunumBi lived deep underground. *They were taking her into their realm!* She knew that once they did, any chance of escape was gone. So she resisted, bucking and swinging her whole body from side to side. It earned her a cuff on the jaw that almost knocked her out.

Through swimming senses Lou saw the stars high above, saw them recede farther and farther as she was carried deeper and deeper into the domain of the demons. Choking back tears, she closed her eyes and did not open them again until much later when the band halted.

A pale glow illuminated their immediate surroundings. Lou saw that it emanated from veins of rock in the wall, veins that gave off a garish green radiance. They were on a broad shelf. From below blew a cool breeze tinged with a foul odor, like that of rotting apples. Some of the NunumBi were conferring, others resting.

Lou was surprised when she was roughly dumped on her back, then ignored as if she were of no consequence. Craning her neck, she couldn't see the stars. She did notice a narrow ledge leading

143

upward and assumed it was the route the creatures had used. Beyond the shelf another ledge wound lower.

Several moved to the edge of the shelf. At a sharp gesture from one, they flattened and peered downward. The others froze.

If Lou hadn't known better, she'd have sworn they were afraid, that below was something capable of scaring even the NunumBi. When the three dwarfs crawled backward from the brink and the whole bunch gathered to confer in excited trills and hisses, she inched forward for a look-see.

Lou really had no notion of what to expect. A tunnel, perhaps. Or a drop-off hundreds of feet high. But before her astounded gaze unfolded a cavern of gigantic proportions, a cavern so vast, all of sprawling St. Louis would fit in it.

Stony spires laced with more glowing veins bathed the cavern in light, intermixed with bizarre and outlandish rock formations of every shape and size. Some were no bigger than a pony; others reared toward the cavern roof like miniature mountains. Lou saw a dark ribbon of water winding across the cavern floor and what might be whitish plants growing along its banks.

"Great God Almighty," Lou breathed. It was a world unto itself, an entire underground domain, existing unsuspected under the very feet of humanity.

Mesmerized by the unearthly splendor, Lou gave a start when something directly below her *moved*. A huge bulk lumbered out of the shadows and stood for a moment close to a spire, the green glow lending it a ghastly hue befitting its ominous presence. It was as tall as two or three men standing on top of one another, with a girth to match. Endowed with bulging muscles, with biceps as thick as barrels and thighs as sturdy as tree trunks, it had a mane of dark shoulder-length hair and wore a loincloth. In one brawny hand was an enormous club.

The shock of seeing it was nothing compared to the shock Lou received when the thing turned toward the shelf and she saw that it had a single large eye in the center of its sloping forehead. Recoiling in terror, she bit her lower lip so she wouldn't scream.

It was madness! Sheer and utter madness! The NunumBi, the

cleft, the cavern, and now the monstrous cyclops! None of it could be real, and yet all of it was. Lou shuddered to think what else might lurk lower down, what other ungodly grotesqueries might prowl the nether realms.

The evidence of her own eyes notwithstanding, Lou pinched herself, hard, in the futile hope it would wake her from the nightmare she was having, that she was really warm and safe under her bedding and not at the threshold to the bowels of the underworld, her life soon to be forfeit.

Hairy hands closed on Lou's ankles and she was violently hauled backward. One of the NunumBi stabbed a finger at her, then at the cavern, then made a hissing sound that Lou interpreted as a warning to stay away from the edge, or else. Or else what? They'd slay her? They were fixing to do that anyway.

"Oh, Zach," Lou said softly, forlornly. "My sweet, wonderful Zach. I'm so sorry. I would have loved to be your wife. Please forgive me." And tears she couldn't deny trickled down her cheeks.

The object of the young woman's devotion was at that moment exerting his tracking skills to their utmost. By torchlight Zach King was following the trail left by his fiancée's captors. Spoor was scant, but there was enough. A heel print there, a scuff mark there. On around the lake he traveled, until he came to a spot where, for no rhyme or reason, the tracks vanished.

Zach lowered the torch. The imprint of a single small foot was clearly embedded, but beyond it the soil was undisturbed. Hunkering, he placed his rifle down to examine the ground. The grass and weeds were much drier and more brittle than they should be, stems snapping at the slightest touch. Puzzled, he poked and prodded, and an entire clump came loose in his hands. Under it, where there should be a shallow hole, was a flat, smooth surface that reminded him of a cured animal hide.

Zach brushed more weeds and grass aside. It *was* a hide, although from no animal he could recognize. His exploring fingertips slid under an edge. Lifting, he discovered a cleft so deep, he couldn't see the bottom when he held the torch in it.

His sister had been telling the truth, Zach realized. This was the spot where she saw the ''little man,'' and the wily NunumBi had taken steps to ensure no one else found it. They were so adept at camouflage, it had fooled even his father.

Rising, Zach pulled and tugged, creating an opening wide enough for him to climb into the cavity. The stygian dark below would intimidate most men, but he never hesitated. Lou was down there somewhere, and he was going to find her.

Zach lay on his belly and swung his legs over the side. Groping for a foothold, he slowly dipped lower until his belt scraped the rim. He was concerned the only way down would be to climb, which he couldn't do holding both the torch and the rifle. Then his left foot scraped against a stone or other projection. He tested it by applying more weight, and it held. Sliding his other leg next to the first, Zach steadied himself and extended the torch as low as he could. To his delight, he was standing on a narrow ledge that angled downward. By moving sideways with his face to the wall, he could go on.

The torch was sputtering. Zach estimated it would hold out another five minutes, maybe ten. After that, he would be as blind as a mole.

A cool but rank breeze rose from the depths. Zach hurried, scraping his rib cage against jutting rocks. It occurred to him that he might be hastening to meet his own death, but he forged on. His pa had once said there were things in life worth dying for, and Louisa certainly qualified. For her sake, for the sake of their love, he would brave any danger, dare any risk.

Hardly a minute elapsed before the ledge widened enough for Zach to walk normally. It wound around bend after bend, and he never knew what awaited him around each turn. The creatures were bound to spy the torchlight, so he had to be ready for anything.

Another minute went by. Two. The cleft was more like a chasm, Zach reflected, a narrow shaft penetrating into a region few men, if any, had ever beheld. But where had the opening come from? It hadn't been there six moons before when he was hunting and passed over that very same stretch of ground. The walls showed no sign of being scraped or nicked by tools or claws, so it was doubtful the NunumBi had dug their way out.

The torch was fading fast, much faster than Zach had anticipated. In anger he shook it, and the shaking brought to mind an incident several months earlier, about the time of the Grass Moon or slightly before. The family had been on their way home from a visit to the Kendall place. Scott Kendall was a good friend of his pa's, a former free trapper who, along with his wife and daughter, lived two days' ride to the south.

On that particular trek back, as Zach recollected, they had been crossing the last high ridge when their horses commenced to act up by nickering and stomping and refusing to go on. Zach had been perplexed by their antics. So had his parents.

Along about then the trees around them began to shake and shimmy. Zach's sorrel had bucked and plunged, almost pitching him off. Intent on staying in the saddle, he'd barely heard a low rumble from deep under the ground. And he hadn't felt the ground itself shake, as his folks said it did.

"That was an earthquake," his father had answered when quizzed by Evelyn "We don't often get them here." His pa had gone on to say that sometimes earthquakes flattened buildings, destroying whole cities. They diverted rivers, split dams.

And if a quake can split a dam, Zach thought, *can't one also split the ground?* Was that how the NunumBi had regained the surface after being gone for so long? Had the earthquake reopened an old 'doorway' to the outer world? If so, it didn't explain the attacks. Did the creatures want his family out of the valley because in ages past it had been part of their territory? Or did the NunumBi relish killing humans on general principle?

So many questions, so few answers.

Zach came to a sharp bend and started around it. The ledge widened again, into a broad shelf. His torch was almost out, but he saw, ahead, on her knees, her wrists and ankles bound, the one he loved. As soon as she saw him, her eyes became saucers.

David Thompson

Overjoyed by his good fortune, Zach sprang toward her. "Lou! They left you here alone? Not so smart, are they?" he crowed.

She sought to speak, but she had been gagged. Tossing her head, she struggled against her bounds like a woman possessed.

"Hold still. I'll have you loose in two shakes of a doe's tail." Zach dropped the torch and whipped out his knife, then saw her eyes stray past him in alarm. Spinning, he learned that he was the one who wasn't so all-fired smart. NunumBi were detaching themselves from nooks and crannies and advancing with claws hooked to rip and rend. They had used Lou as bait and he had walked right into their trap.

Zach would acquit himself as a Shoshone warrior should. Planting himself in front of Lou, he raised his rifle.

Minutes earlier, Louisa had swiped at her eyes and squared her shoulders. Some of the creatures were looking at her, and she refused to weep in front of them. They might take pleasure in her misery, and she would not give them the satisfaction.

Three NunumBi, maybe the same three as before, crawled to the edge of the shelf to gaze into the cavern.

Lou gathered that they were so worried by the ogre with the club, they wouldn't move on until it was gone. She smiled. It gave *her* satisfaction to know there was something the NunumBi feared. It also gave her an idea. An insane idea that might get her killed but also might grant her an opportunity to escape.

Sitting up, Lou rested her chin on a knee and closed her eyes as if she were distraught. But her eyes were open a crack, her legs coiled for what she had to do. She watched the trio who were watching the ogre, and when they slid back and rose to rejoin their fellows, she hurled herself at the edge, rising to her full height and cupping both hands to her mouth.

Lou's aim was to shout at the top of her lungs to get the giant's attention. To lure it to the shelf. Either the NunumBi would battle the cyclops and possibly perish, or they would retreat back up the cleft to the surface. Either way, the confusion might permit her to flee.

But Lou hadn't reckoned on their uncanny quickness. The three who had been spying on the giant were on her as she raised her hands. One executed an amazing leap and smothered her outcry, while the others seized her about the waist and legs. She was slammed onto her side, the blow jarring her spine and whooshing the air from her lungs.

Claws lanced at her throat but stopped a pine needle's width shy of sinking into her flesh. All the NunumBi were clustered around her, and Lou sensed her reprieve would be short-lived, that many of them would like to slay her right there for what she had just done. In that terrifying moment when her life hung in the balance, a hideous roar swelled from the immense cavern and snapped up the heads of the NunumBi.

Two dashed to the brink, crouched, and looked. Whatever they saw had them back in a twinkling. A rapid exchange of guttural sounds resulted in Lou's being seized. Before she could comprehend what they were up to, they had ripped lengths of buckskin from her shirt and were binding her wrists and ankles.

Lou fought, but she was a sparrow against hawks. A surly creature ripped off another strip and attempted to shove it into her mouth. When she bit at his fingers, another grasped her jaw and forced her mouth wide so the gag could be stuffed in. Seized by the elbows, she was dragged to the middle of the shelf. Then, like rabbits melting into high grass, the NunumBi disappeared into cracks and crevices lining the wall.

Why had they left her there, helpless and alone? The answer to Lou's unvoiced query came in the form of another hideous roar, closer than before. The monster had seen her and was on its way up! Frantic, she rubbed her wrists and ankles back and forth, but the creatures had tied her too well. She would never free herself before the ogre arrived.

A pair of red eyes gleamed at her from a crack. Lou kicked a rock at it, a childish act born of fury. She cocked her head, listening for the giant. Footsteps from the other direction went unnoticed until the person making them was halfway across the shelf.

It was Zach! Lou's heart swelled, then instantly constricted as his peril sank home. She fought to warn him, to spit out the gag or loosen her hands, but could do neither. His knife flashed out and so did the NunumBi, converging on her beloved from all sides as he took a stand in front of her. Never had she been prouder of him. But pride without life was as worthless as fool's gold, and they both might lose theirs, either to the scarlet-eyed devils who ringed them or to the massive behemoth clomping steadily upward.

Zach King heard the heavy tread of gigantic feet but had no time to speculate on the source. The NunumBi had him surrounded and were closing in, their claws hooked, their rapier teeth bared. He sighted down the Hawken and at point-blank range shot one in the face, the impact flinging it over the edge of the shelf.

A thunderous boom reverberated, echoing again and again into the distance. Zach snatched at a pistol, but as he did the creatures were on him, tearing the knife from his grasp, pinning his arms and locking his legs. They brought him crashing down with half of them on top. The dwarf holding his left arm let go to scrabble out from under the heap, and Zach punched one straddling his chest. Claws closed on his neck and glittering teeth arced toward his throat.

Lou screeched, or tried to. Her sweetheart was about to die, and she couldn't lift a finger to help him. Or could she? Her ankles were bound, but she could still move her legs. Swiveling on her rear and tucking her knees to her chest, she drove both feet into the head of the creature on Zach's chest. It tumbled, and Lou drew her legs up to kick another. She didn't see where the NunumBi who pounced on her came from, but suddenly she was on her left side with a dwarf perched on her shoulder and claws rising toward her jugular.

Zach was fighting for all he was worth, punching, gouging, kicking. His blows, though, had no effect, other than to make the creatures mad. Again he was smashed flat, his wrists seized as if in iron clamps. Another dwarf took the place of the one Lou had kicked, its hairy hands reaching for him. This time Lou couldn't help. This time he would die.

Twisting his neck, Zach saw one of the little brutes about to rip Lou open. "Nooooo!" he cried, heaving upward in boiling wrath. But the NunumBi were not to be denied, and held him down.

It was then, with both of them moments away from grisly ends, that a horrendous roar seemed to shake the very shelf. The NunumBi glanced toward the other end, where the ledge continued downward. Snarls and growls burst from them in a bestial chorus, as, bristling, they charged.

Zach rolled onto his stomach to push himself erect. He glimpsed *something* that filled the opening past the shelf, something gigantic. It was in shadow and he couldn't view it all that well, nor did he waste precious seconds trying. Whatever it was, it was a godsend, for the NunumBi had temporarily forgotten all about Lou and him. Scrambling onto his knees, he pried at the knots on her wrists, then spotted his knife lying close by. Two slashes made short shrift of the buckskin. Two more freed her ankles. As he pulled her up, she yanked the gag out.

"Run, dearest! Run!"

Zach started to sprint toward the ledge that would take them to the surface. Remembering his rifle and other pistol, he veered to claim them, but Lou wrenched on his arm, nearly yanking him off his feet.

"No! Forget them! Just run!" Lou pleaded. "For God's sake, run!" The unholy din behind them had reached earsplitting proportions, roars and shrieks and howls in riotous bedlam.

Zach wasn't inclined to do any such thing. Guns were too valuable. No Shoshone warrior would leave one on the field of battle, no mountaineer would give his up unless it was pried from his lifeless, cold fingers. He resisted her pull, saying, "We need them!"

"Please! Let's go while we can!" Lou dug in her heels.

Stunned that she would dispute him when he knew what was best, Zach gripped her arm to drag her if need be. Out of the corner of an eye he saw a war being waged, the dwarfs thronging around the giant in the shadows, slashing and rending in fierce abandon. One was circling, seeking an opening, when an enormous club crashed onto its head, shattering bones and pulverizing flesh, crushing the creature to a miserable, wretched pulp.

Zach reversed direction, and Lou fell into step beside him. His father always kept a spare rifle handy. He'd use that until he could buy or trade for a new one of his own. Coming to the ledge, he glanced over a shoulder to see how the NunumBi were faring.

Not well. More than half had met the same fate as their companion, their ruined bodies reduced to gory smears. Yet the remainder fought on, berserk bloodlust driving them to a frenzy.

Zach saw the giant clearly for a second and refused to believe his own eyes. He decided that he couldn't have seen what he thought he did. The NunumBi alone were enough to stretch a person's sanity to breaking point. The apparition towering above them was madness run rampant.

Rounding the first bend, Zach had to slow down. They had no torch, no means to light their way, and inky blackness enveloped them like a shroud. Lou's fingers dug into his palm, and she glued herself to him. "Don't worry. We'll make it," he said, facing the wall and groping upward.

Lou wanted to hug him, to smother him with kisses. "You came for me," she marveled. "You really came for me."

"Why are you so surprised?" Zach said. "Did you think I wouldn't?" Females could be so silly. "I love you, don't I?"

Lou's mother used to say that love was like a well in that the truer it was, the deeper it ran. She had proof of that now, and her heart filled with happiness that eclipsed any she had ever felt. Her whole body grew warm, her urge to kiss him nigh overwhelming. "I am yours forever," she declared.

"That's nice," Zach absently replied. Women picked the darnedest times to be romantic. He concentrated on their ascent, moving each foot with care so they didn't pitch into the abyss. By his reckoning they should almost be to the next bend.

"Listen!" Lou exclaimed.

The clamor of combat had ceased. In the dreadful stillness new sounds could be heard: the ponderous thump of huge feet drawing steadily closer.

Chapter Twelve

Louisa May Clark thought she knew what fear was. She thought her ordeal with the NunumBi had taught her what it was like to be so overcome by fright, she couldn't think straight. But she had been wrong. It was possible to be even more scared, to be so frightened that every breath caught in her throat and her heart hammered against her chest as if trying to burst out.

Being deprived of the sense of sight was bad enough. Not being able to see, having to inch upward with a yawning chasm at her back, aware that a single misstep would plummet her to a gruesome end, was scary enough. But to have a monster at her back, a living, wheezing abomination that craved to crush her as it had the dwarfs, compounded her fear a hundredfold. She clung to Zach with one hand while clinging to the wall with the other, gradually working higher. "We'll never make it." The darkness forced them to move too slowly. Eventually the ogre was bound to catch up.

"Don't give up," Zach said. It was one of the most important lessons his parents taught him, a virtue impressed on him again and again. Never, ever, give up hope. Hardships were challenges to be met and bested. In the wilderness, the true measure of a person was not in how strong they were, or how quick, or even how smart, but in their single-minded will to survive.

To their rear the tread of giant feet was replaced by a scuffling noise. It was no coincidence that the ledge had narrowed. Their gargantuan pursuer was now doing the same as they were, shuffling upward one stride at a time so as not to lose its balance.

"That thing is moving slower," Lou whispered.

So were they. Zach had to reach forward, grip the wall, then slide his legs up the incline while keeping his other hand wrapped around her wrist. Then she would do the same. When their shoulders touched, he would reach forward again.

How long they climbed, Zach couldn't say. By degrees the scuffling grew louder, ever louder, and at length Zach could hear raspy breathing that sounded more like a blacksmith's bellows than the lungs of a living being.

Lou looked back frequently. Several times she saw movement in the murk, or imagined she did. She also thought she saw the abomination's pale skin. "If we don't get out of this alive—" she began to say.

"We will," Zach cut her off.

"Maybe. But if we don't, I want to say how much your love has meant to me. If I must die, I can't think of a better way than at your side."

Zach didn't like to talk about dying. The idea of losing her was unbearable. So he changed the subject. "After we go around the next bend, I want you to slide past me. Take the lead."

"Why? Your eyesight is better than mine," Lou observed. He could pick out objects at a great distance, like an eagle, and always spotted elk, deer, and whatnot long before she did. Ideally, he should be in front.

"I still have one pistol left," Zach noted. "If need be, I can hold that thing back, delay it long enough for you to get away."

"A cannon couldn't stop it," Lou declared. "No, we should keep going just as we are. I'd be too afraid of slipping and causing us both to fall."

Zach had to come up with another reason. In truth, he didn't want her behind him because the monstrosity would grab her first. Extending his left arm, he felt empty space. By bending his elbow he established that another bend had to be negotiated. "Careful," he said. "Another turn."

The ledge was no wider than his foot. Zach pressed his moccasins flush with the wall and inched ahead. As his stomach scraped the edge, he happened to gaze into the gloom past his betrothed and spied a hulking shape climbing toward them. The giant had to be clinging to the ledge by its toes, yet it was moving at twice their speed. They'd never reach the surface unless he could slow the thing down.

Zach moved another yard, giving Lou room to maneuver around the bend. Once she did, he hugged the wall and said urgently, "It's now or never. Slide on past me. Hurry."

"You're doing it for my sake," Lou answered. "And I refuse to be coddled. I'm not your little sister."

In all the months they'd been together, Zach had never done what he did now. Squeezing her wrist, he said sternly, "Listen to me, damn it! Do as I say!"

To Lou, it was the same as if he'd slapped her. He'd never used that tone before, never been so outright bossy. She had the right to do as she pleased, and she wouldn't allow anyone, not even the one she loved, to order her to do otherwise. "No." If one of them must sacrifice their life to buy the other some time for the other to get away, she was perfectly willing to make the sacrifice herself.

Zach faced a dilemma. His father had brought him up to believe that no man worthy of the name ran roughshod over a woman. He knew of some husbands, Shoshones and whites alike, who treated their wives worse than they did their horses, who were always telling their womenfolk to do this or do that. A few men regularly beat their women, slapping them around if their wives didn't do exactly as they wanted when they wanted. Long ago Zach had made up his mind that he would never be like those men. He would be like his pa.

But now, with the giant narrowing the gap and their lives in the balance, Zach was put to the test. He could let Lou have her way, in which case she would be the first one the ogre slew. Or he could try to save her in spite of herself. Which to do?

"I'm sorry," Zach said. His left hand had found a knobby stone he could hold on to, and grasping it securely, he suddenly pulled Louisa toward him, looped his other arm around her waist, and partly pushed, partly swung her behind him so she'd have no choice but to go on past.

Lou nearly screamed. For harrowing heartbeats she hung half over the edge, held in place only by Zach's arm and the balls of her feet. She clutched at him, then realized she might tear him from their roost. Her only other recourse was to throw herself to the left, beyond him, and lever against the wall to keep from keeling backward. Panting from the exertion as much as her panic, she exclaimed, "You almost killed us!"

Louder breathing than hers motivated Zach to give her a light push. "Keep going! Don't look back!"

"What—?" Lou was mad now—mad he had made her do as he wanted against her will, mad at his lack of respect for her wishes.

"Go!" Zach shouted, but it was too late, for at the bend materialized a huge, pale bulk, looming above them like a sequoia. A gigantic hand reached for him, fingers as thick as his wrist seeking to enclose him in their steely fold. Forgetting himself, he jerked away, lost his grip, and started to fall.

Now Lou did scream. Lunging, she snagged his arm and pulled him back. Breath unspeakably foul assailed them, almost making her gag. She looked up, up, up, into a ghastly visage, into an eye as wide around as an apple, at a hooked nose and a slavering mouth the size of a pie plate. The great eye blinked as the giant regarded them with interest.

Zach didn't bother looking up. His only thought was that Lou was about to be slain. Twisting so he could unlimber his pistol, he pointed it at the creature's chest, at where he hoped the heart would be, and fired.

An unearthly howl resounded in the chasm, a cry as horrid as its maker, a piercing, blood-chilling mix of pain and rage. The giant grabbed at its chest, teetered, and slid into the void.

Zach hadn't expected it to be so easy. Momentarily blinded by the muzzle flash, he blinked to clear his vision and listened for the crash of the huge body far, far below. Instead he heard more heavy wheezing. As his eyes adjusted to the darkness, he made out the giant's pale figure, hanging by both massive hands from the ledge. While Zach looked on, the monster started to hike itself back onto the ledge.

"Move!" Zach urged, propelling Lou upward.

She didn't argue. The ogre would be after them in earnest. It was a race to the surface, and the giant had the advantage because this was its domain. It could see well despite the lack of light. It was accustomed to traveling subterranean byways. Then Lou had a thought. They need not climb all the way. Higher up, the cleft narrowed, and the monster would be unable to follow. She mentioned as much.

Zach peered upward, seeking some hint of stars and sky, but there was none. They hurried, moving as fast as was humanly possible, much faster than it was safe to do, but it was either push recklessly on or be reduced to a bloody smear, as the NunumBi had been.

No sound of pursuit arose, which puzzled Zach. He hoped against hope the giant had slipped and fallen, but the more likely explanation was that the thing was badly wounded and couldn't move as swiftly.

Long, anxious minutes dragged by, weighted by millstones. Lou began to flag. Her legs were aching, her calf and thigh muscles terribly sore. Yet another bend brought them to a straight section that angled more steeply than any. Weary, she tilted her head back to relieve a cramp in her neck, and halted.

"Look!"

A patch of stars sparkled, beckoning like a lighthouse in a fog, promising safety if they could only reach the top. Zach leaned against the wall, his ears primed for the slightest noise. He couldn't hear anything over Lou's gasps. "We'll rest a little bit," he said.

Lou noted that the opposite wall was ten to twelve feet distant, more than enough room for the ogre. "Maybe it's not coming. Maybe you killed it."

"Maybe," Zach said. She was grasping at a straw, and they both knew it.

They fell quiet, but the eerie silence of the netherworld made Lou nervous, so she brought up the first notion that entered her head: "What will the Shoshones do when they learn about the NunumBi? Wage war on them like their ancestors did?"

Zach would like that. The glory of counting coup on the fierce dwarfs would exceed any other courageous feat a warrior could perform. A NunumBi scalp would earn its owner prestige and fame beyond his wildest dreams.

"What about your family? How can you go on living in the valley, never knowing what might crawl out of this hole next?"

"We'll never give up our home," Zach said. "Never."

Lou's fingers were entwined with his, and she gently rubbed a fingertip across his palm. "Will it be our home, too, once we're married? Or will we go find a nice valley of our own? Maybe that grassy one north of here, with the stream and the meadow where the elk always are? It would be a perfect spot to raise kids."

The workings of the female mind never failed to astound Zach. Here they were, being hunted by a creature from the dawn of time, balanced on a small ledge above a yawning chasm, and she was rambling about where they would build their cabin and the children they would have? His uncle Shakespeare once said that women were proof the Almighty had a sense of humor, and Zach now believed he understood what Shakespeare meant.

"I wish we were already man and wife," Lou remarked. For what he had done, for braving the dangers of the depths to save her, he deserved to be rewarded as only a woman could reward a man. Lou blushed, glad he couldn't see. She was behaving like a wanton, yet she couldn't deny her feelings. She wanted him, wanted him so very much.

"Maybe it will be sooner than you think," Zach said. His whole outlook had changed. He was no longer content to wait, not when he could lose her at any time. If not to the NunumBi, then to roving Blackfeet or a grizzly or a hundred and one other dangers. He would discuss it with his pa—if they lived that long.

"Did you just hear something?" Lou asked.

Zach bent an ear lower. No, he hadn't heard a thing. But then the faint scrape of a foot or an arm alerted him to a moving mass below. It was the giant. The monster wasn't using the ledge anymore, as they were. It was climbing *straight up the wall*, straight up the side of the cleft, a great, pale spider, exhibiting an agility belied by its bulk.

Lou tugged on his arm. "Oh, Lord!"

"Go!" Zach said. "Go! Go! Go!"

They continued their ascent. And if they had been reckless before, they were doubly so now. Yet the monster rapidly gained. Zach stopped looking back and goaded Lou to go even faster. Ahead was one more turn. If Zach's memory served, once they were past it the cleft narrowed to less than three feet. The giant would be stymied and couldn't climb any higher.

Lou was only a few feet from the bend when a loud grunt drew her gaze under them. The ogre was almost within reach. It had caught them unawares and was elevating a huge hand. "Zach! Below you!"

The warning came a split second too late. Blunt fingers wrapped around Zach's left shin and he was brought up short. The giant pulled, nearly dislodging him. He had little to hold on to other than a crack at shoulder height, so kicking with his other foot was out of the question. But he still had his pistol, and, shifting, he hurled it at the leering face. More by accident than design, he struck it in the eye.

Howling in torment, the creature let go.

Zach and Lou scurried around the turn and on up the ledge. Fresh air blew on their sweaty skin. The tops of trees waved above the opening. They were close to the opening, so tantalizingly close.

Lou stumbled, but Zach held on to her and helped her stand. "Just a little further," he coaxed.

Suddenly the entire cleft shook to an immense impact. Drooling spittle and roaring, the giant had flung itself into the cramped space like a living battering ram. The walls held, preventing him from climbing any higher, but they didn't deter him. Lashed by rampant fury, it attacked the two walls, pounding off large chunks with powerful blows and digging deep furrows with iron nails.

"Nothing will stop it!" Lou exclaimed.

Zach had witnessed beasts and men in the grip of bloodlust, but never a rage to rival this. The creature would not be denied. Slowly but inevitably it was forcing itself upward. His arm over Lou's shoulder, he guided her toward the highest point they could reach, which was still three feet under the rim.

The giant tried a new tactic. Rocks and globs of dirt pelted the wall around them, most barely missing.

A stone stung Zach's shoulder, and he winced. Another gashed his thigh. Their nemesis was trying to knock them off the ledge, to make them fall into its waiting arms. But they were almost there! Another six or seven steps and they would reach the end.

As if it divined their intent, the ogre started heaving heavy rocks above them, at the ledge itself. Large pieces were broken off and rained down on them, forcing them to cover their heads with their arms for protection. When the giant stopped, Zach glanced up and discovered much of the ledge was gone. They could go another yard or so, but that was all. And they wouldn't be high enough to reach the rim. Their escape had been cut off.

The creature resumed its onslaught on the walls, widening the cleft so it could get at them. Its huge hands were like twin shovels. At the rate it was digging, in several minutes they would be at its mercy.

"What do we do?" Louisa asked. She couldn't think of a thing.

"Try climbing." Zach stretched and sought handholds, but the few he could reach wouldn't bear his weight. He braced a hand

and a foot against the other wall and tried to pump upward, but now the walls were so close together he couldn't make full use of his upper arms and kept slipping.

Lou was terrified he would fall. "Don't try that!" she said, ready to grab hold if he should lose his grip.

A lancing pang in his lower leg gave Zach another reason to stop. The creature had thrown a rock at him. It was determined to keep them right where they were. Zach dropped back onto the ledge.

"I'm sorry," Lou said, embracing him. She blamed herself for the fix they were in. Had she been more vigilant back at the cabin, the NunumBi might not have abducted her and Zach wouldn't be about to lose his life. "It's going to get us."

Not if Zach could help it. There was one ploy left to them, one he would rather not resort to, but which he would unhesitatingly do if there were no other means of saving Louisa. As strong as the monster was, he doubted it could retain its grip were he to jump from the ledge on top of it. He'd crash onto its head and shoulders, tear it from its precarious perch, and send them both hurtling into the bowels of the earth. His life would be forfeit, but Lou would be spared, and to Zach that was all that counted.

Lou pressed her warm lips to his. "I love you, Stalking Coyote."

"And I love you." Zach gazed into her lovely eyes for what would be the final time. She mustn't suspect, or she would seek to stop him. "Never forget that. Not for as long as you live."

"As long as I—?" Lou said. Something in his voice, in his eyes, spiked dread through her and she held him close. The giant was clawing higher, but she didn't care. She molded herself to her betrothed and gave him a kiss to end all kisses.

Zach couldn't delay another moment. The brute would soon reach them. Gently prying Lou off, he gloried in the beauty of her features, then abruptly took a step back, turned, and pressed a hand against the wall to push off.

"What are you *doing*?"

Just as Zach shoved, Lou grabbed him. They teetered outward, above the creature, and would have dropped had Zach not slammed both hands against the other wall and pushed them back onto the ledge.

Lou clung to him, quaking uncontrollably. "No, no, no." She realized what he had been about to do, and the depth of his sacrifice moved her to tears. "I would rather die with you than go on living without you."

Zach was too choked up to speak. He had to save her in spite of herself. He could still shove her, then jump. But knowing her, she'd probably leap after him. The only way to ensure she didn't was to punch her on the jaw, to daze her long enough for him to accomplish what had to be done. But then she might fall.

"Did you hear me?" Lou asked, afraid he would try again.

Barely. The giant's bellows and growls, the scrape of its nails, the pounding of its mallet fists, nearly drowned her out. Zach smiled, even as he bunched his right fist. He must act quickly, before he changed his mind.

Light suddenly bathed the cleft. Squinting up, Zach saw a pair of silhouettes framed by a blazing torch. "Grab hold of this! We'll pull you up!" someone hollered. His pa, he thought.

"Grab hold of what?" Lou said.

Into the cleft dropped a rope. It dangled in front of them, within easy reach, and Zach snagged it. "You first," he said.

Unwilling to leave him, Lou balked. "What about you?"

"They can't lift us both at the same time," Zach noted. "Now, hurry!" Shoving the rope into her hands, he tugged, then shouted, "Pull, Pa, pull! She's ready!" He stepped back as Lou fairly flew toward the rim, swinging like a pendulum. Her legs clipped him on the shoulder, and he had to gouge his fingers into the wall to keep from doing what he had been intent on doing just a minute before.

A shriek ripped from the giant. It saw its quarry eluding it and redoubled its frenzied efforts.

Relief washed over Zach like spring rain as Lou was hauled out of the cleft to safety. He sidled to the end of the ledge to wait for the rope to be thrown back down. By now the creature was so close it could almost seize him, but it had slowed, squinting against the torchlight. Like the NunumBi, a lifetime of underground existence had rendered its eye sensitive to bright light.

A gigantic hand groped upward. Zach had gone as far as he could, and he watched in helpless fascination as its thick fingers made contact with the ledge and probed over the lip, questing for his legs. They were six inches away, then five, then four. He started when something hit him across the shoulder and chest, and swatting at it, he saw it was the rope.

"Hold on, son! We'll get you out of there!"

Zach gripped it tightly. "Now, Pa!" The giant's hand was an inch from his foot. As he rose, a finger brushed against his ankle. Instantly, the giant grabbed at his leg but narrowly missed. "Faster, Pa, or I'm a goner!"

The rope shot upward. Zach knew his father was strong, but he never imagined his pa could lift him as if he weighed no more than a feather. Another colossal roar thundered as he rose clear of the rim and was dragged a dozen feet. Strong hands raised him by his shoulders, and he turned, smiling, expecting his father. But it was someone else. "Touch the Clouds!" he blurted.

The tall Shoshone was haggard and worn, his buckskins streaked with grime. Clapping Zach on the back, he said in his own tongue, "Finding you alive makes my heart glad, Stalking Coyote."

"But how did you get here? Where did you come from?" Of all the warriors in the tribe, Zach had always admired Touch the Clouds most.

"It is a story for later," the living legend said.

Nate and Winona came from the shadows. Evelyn, holding the torch, was backing away from the opening. "Your sister heard you leave and woke us up," his father revealed. "Touch the Clouds showed up as we were coming after you. Good thing that we did."

Louisa darted to Zach, flinging her arms around his neck. "We're safe now, darling! We've nothing to worry about!"

As if to prove her wrong, the ground around the cleft heaved and a gargantuan arm flailed skyward. The giant commenced tearing out clods of earth to make the opening wide enough to clamber out.

Evelyn screeched and ran to her mother. "What is it, Ma? What is that thing?"

"Give me a gun!" Zach said. "We can't let it reach the surface!"

Nate flung the rope down and ran toward the monstrosity, yelling, "Get them out of here, Winona! Take cover!"

Winona did as she was bid. The girls and Touch the Clouds trailed her, but not Zach. He hadn't deserted Lou, he wouldn't desert his father. "Pa! You can't fight that thing!" Zach had no weapons other than his knife, which he whipped out as he broke into a run. His father didn't realize what they were up against. Zach had to get him out of there before the giant broke through.

At the west end of the cleft, Nate squatted. From his possibles bag he quickly took his fire steel and flint.

"Pa, you don't know what you're doing," Zach said, hunkering beside him. The ogre's arm was only a couple of yards away, clawing at the soil, the monster rumbling like a steam engine. "We have to—" Zach began, then saw what his father was doing. Sparks leaped, igniting thin lines of black powder, and flames and smoke flashed toward kegs that had been wedged into the cleft. "Oh, Lordy."

Nate rose, grasped his son, and hurtled toward the pines. He had a log already picked out, and, practically heaving Zach behind it, he dived flat just as the kegs went up. The explosion was everything he had hoped it would be. Tons of dirt and rock spewed into the air as the ground underneath shuddered, then the debris cascaded down onto the cleft, which was collapsing in on itself. An earsplitting shrick was smothered by the titanic blast. Nate didn't move until the last of the earth and stones showered down, until the ground subsided and the dust thinned. He was caked with dirt and stinging from bruises. Coughing, he swatted at particles hanging in the air, and slowly stood.

"You did it, Pa," Zach said, not quite able to grasp that they had really been saved. It had happened so fast.

The cleft was no more. The entrance to the netherworld had been obliterated. A mound of dirt and stones would serve as a lasting marker—and a lasting warning.

Winona brought Evelyn and Lou into the open. Giggling, the girls clasped each other and danced in a circle.

Touch the Clouds joined them, raising his hands to the heavens and beginning a singsong chant. He was thanking Apo for their deliverance, and for his own, when the NunumBi chased him into that tree, and he had spent the night in the highest branches he could reach, the creatures prowling below until the crack of dawn.

Nate looked at his son. He should be mad, he should punish Zach for disobeying and going off alone. But he had to remember that Zach was on the verge of manhood, and no man would have done differently when the life of the woman he loved was at stake. "*We* did it," he amended.

Winona was glad it was finished. Their lives could return to normal. Their valley, their home, was safe. "The terror is over," she said in Shoshone, and her husband, her son, and her daughter all looked at her and smiled.

Touch the Clouds stopped singing. He had not told them yet about Old Charlie Walker. They were so happy, so relieved, he was reluctant to bring them bad tidings. But they had to know, they had to be warned. He cleared his throat.

Afterword

Transcribing the King journals presents unusual challenges.

Most entries detail the day-to-day life of an average mountain man, or mountaineer, as they liked to call themselves. Dramatic moments, such as clashes with unfriendly tribes, encounters with vicious whites, and conflicts with savage beasts, have formed the crux of the Wilderness series. I have done my best to retell them as faithfully as possible, to relate them as stories you might hear were you seated around a roaring campfire with those who experienced them.

But what are we to make of the more sensational entries? The hairy man-beasts Nate battled in Wilderness #9? The time he says he was sucked up into a tornado and lived? The lost valley in Wilderness #23? And now the NunumBi?

Did the events occur as Nate King recorded them? Or was he "pulling our leg"? Mountain men were notorious for telling tall tales. Bridger, Meek, Russell, they all enjoyed swapping yarns to see who could outdo the other. Are some of Nate King's entries in the same vein?

Ultimately, you, the reader, must decide.

David Thompson

What do I believe? I try to stay impartial, but some of the accounts do strain belief. There are a few I've hesitated to transcribe for that very reason.

But who knows. Perhaps one day you'll read about his run-in with the "red-headed cannibals" of Shoshone legend. Or that lake, high in the Rockies, where a water beast lurks. Or the great bear, the last of its kind, that decapitated buffalo with a swipe of a paw.

Time will tell.

WILDERNESS

#27
GOLD RAGE

DAVID THOMPSON

Penniless old trapper Ben Frazier is just about ready to pack it all in when an Arapaho warrior takes pity on him and shows him where to find the elusive gold that white men value so greatly. His problems seem to be over, but then another band of trappers finds out about the gold and forces Ben to lead them to it. It's up to Zach King to save the old man, but can he survive a fight against a gang of gold-crazed mountain men?

___4519-2 $3.99 US/$4.99 CAN

Dorchester Publishing Co., Inc.
P.O. Box 6640
Wayne, PA 19087-8640

WILDERNESS

BLOOD FEUD

David Thompson

The brutal wilderness of the Rocky Mountains can be deadly to those unaccustomed to its dangers. So when a clan of travelers from the hill country back East arrive at Nate King's part of the mountain, Nate is more than willing to lend a hand and show them some hospitality. He has no way of knowing that this clan is used to fighting—and killing—for what they want. And they want Nate's land for their own!

___4477-3 $3.99 US/$4.99 CAN

WILDERNESS

#25
FRONTIER
MAYHEM

<—————————————————————>

David Thompson

The unforgiving wilderness of the Rocky Mountains forces a boy to grow up fast, so Nate King taught his son, Zach, how to survive the constant hazards and hardships—and he taught him well. With an Indian war party on the prowl and a marauding grizzly on the loose, young Zach is about to face the test of his life, with no room for failure. But there is one danger Nate hasn't prepared Zach for—a beautiful girl with blue eyes.

___4433-1 $3.99 US/$4.99 CAN

Dorchester Publishing Co., Inc.
P.O. Box 6640
Wayne, PA 19087-8640

Please add $1.75 for shipping and handling for the first book and $.50 for each book thereafter. NY, NYC, and PA residents, please add appropriate sales tax. No cash, stamps, or C.O.D.s. All orders shipped within 6 weeks via postal service book rate. Canadian orders require $2.00 extra postage and must be paid in U.S. dollars through a U.S. banking facility.

Name_____
Address_____
City_____ State_____ Zip_____
I have enclosed $_____ in payment for the checked book(s).
Payment <u>must</u> accompany all orders. ❑ Please send a free catalog.
CHECK OUT OUR WEBSITE! www.dorchesterpub.com

WILDERNESS

#24

Mountain Madness

⟷

David Thompson

When Nate King comes upon a pair of green would-be trappers from New York, he is only too glad to risk his life to save them from a Piegan war party. It is only after he takes them into his own cabin that he realizes they will repay his kindness...with betrayal. When the backshooters reveal their true colors, Nate knows he is in for a brutal battle—with the lives of his family hanging in the balance.

___4399-8 $3.99 US/$4.99 CAN

Dorchester Publishing Co., Inc.
P.O. Box 6640
Wayne, PA 19087-8640

WILDERNESS

TRAPPER'S BLOOD/ MOUNTAIN CAT

DAVID THOMPSON

Trapper's Blood. In the wild Rockies, a man has to act as judge, jury, and executioner against his enemies. And when trappers start turning up dead, their bodies horribly mutilated, Nate King and his friends vow to hunt down the ruthless killers. But taking the law into their own hands, they soon find out that a hasty decision can make them as guilty as the murderers they want to stop.

And in the same action-packed volume...

Mountain Cat. A seasoned hunter and trapper, Nate King can fend off attacks from brutal warriors and furious grizzlies alike. But a hunt for a mountain lion twice the size of other deadly cats proves to be his greatest challenge. If Nate can't destroy the monstrous creature, it will slaughter innocent settlers—and the massacre might well begin with Nate's own family!

____4621-0 $4.99 US/$5.99 CAN

Dorchester Publishing Co., Inc.
P.O. Box 6640
Wayne, PA 19087-8640